The Cat and the Jill of Diamonds

A Midnight Louie Las Vegas Adventure

Book 3

Other Five Star Titles
by Carole Nelson Douglas:

The Cat and the King of Clubs
The Cat and the Queen of Hearts

The Cat and the Jill of Diamonds

A Midnight Louie Las Vegas Adventure

Book 3

CAROLE NELSON DOUGLAS

Five Star
Unity, Maine

Five Star First Edition Mystery Series.
Published in 2000 in conjunction with Tekno Books
and Ed Gorman.

Set in 11 pt. Plantin by Minnie B. Raven.

Printed in the United States on permanent paper.

Library of Congress Cataloging-in-Publication Data

Douglas, Carole Nelson.
    The cat and the Jill of diamonds / by Carole Nelson Douglas.
        p.   cm.—(A Midnight Louie Las Vegas adventure ; bk. 3)
    ISBN 0-7862-2540-8 (hc : alk. paper)
    1. Midnight Louie (Fictitious character)—Fiction.
2. Las Vegas (Nev.)—Fiction.   3. Cats—Fiction.   I. Title.
PS3554.O8237 C23   2000
813′.54—dc21   00-024316

♦ Author's Foreword ♦

This is the third of the short novels comprising the Midnight Louie Quartet. These books—written in 1985–86 and finally published two to a paperback-original volume as *Crystal Days* and *Crystal Nights* in 1990, have been out of print until now, and have never before been available in hardcover editions.

They introduced feline sleuth Midnight Louie, whose current mystery series has eleven books in print: *Catnap, Pussyfoot, Cat on a Blue Monday, Cat in a Crimson Haze, Cat in a Diamond Dazzle, Cat with an Emerald Eye, Cat in a Flamingo Fedora, Cat in a Golden Garland, Cat in a Hyacinth Hunt, Cat in an Indigo Mood, Cat in a Jeweled Jumpsuit,* and *Cat in a Kiwi Con.* The interior alphabet that began with *Blue Monday* means that this series will ultimately number 27 books.

This current Midnight Louie mystery series shares the same Las Vegas setting as the earlier books, but reflects the city's incredible building boom of the past 15 years (to which I have added fictional hotel-casinos, like the Crystal Phoenix and the Goliath that feature in the Quartet and in the subsequent series). Many of the secondary characters and backgrounds from the Quartet also feature in the current series, forming a continuing universe, and the Quartet is the entire reason the Midnight Louie mystery series exists at all.

When the Quartet was sold to a category romance editor in 1985, it was one of the first limited series within a romance "line," and was the first to include crime and mystery elements (not to mention the first to feature a feline PI narrator), anticipating trends that have become bestsellers since then.

The romance editor enthusiastically bought the Quartet and received the first MS. Then something happened.

The books were held from publication for four years, so long that the contract expired. During that time, I was promised various publishing dates and methods of publishing—the first book in hardcover, for instance—that never came about. A clue to the delay was in the editor's description of the books: "too mainstream, upmarket, and sophisticated" for romance readers. Finally, the editor promised that the books would be well published and I would be pleased, and that they would be out within a year.

They came out in the summer of 1990, not in the romance line, but as midlist romances. And I was not pleased. The editor had crammed the four books into two paperbacks containing two stories each. The 120,000-word length of the doubled-up books wasn't economical, so the editor cut each book up to 37 percent without my knowledge or participation. (I call this approach "cutting the body to fit the coffin.")

I wouldn't have seen galley proofs had I not asked for them, and did all I could then to salvage the books. They did not meet my standards: plot elements seemed pulled out of the blue without preparation; mystery elements and deeper characterizations were stripped out, as were secondary characters. The Midnight Louie sections were cut forty percent.

I was convinced that the very elements the romance editor found "too upmarket, mainstream, and sophisticated"—Midnight Louie's narration, the Las Vegas setting, and the mystery/romance blend—were strengths, not weaknesses. So I "flipped" the concept and took Louie to the mystery side of the street, where he has been welcome indeed. Midnight Louie, after all, is based on a real alley cat with awesome survival skills. He weighed eighteen pounds from eating a California motel's decorative goldfish, which almost got him sent to the animal Death Row before a cat-lover flew him to her home fifteen hundred miles away to save him.

I am grateful for the reader interest that makes it possible for the Midnight Louie Quartet to return in a restored form the author can endorse. In preparing the four novels for republication, I restored material that had been cut, including all of Louie's narrative sections. These were always briefer than they are in the current mystery series. Just having a cat narrator was daring enough in 1985–86; I had to keep his contributions short, if not sweet. Since the books were written as romances first, the mystery/crime elements are lighter than in the mystery series, but they involve a continuing puzzle that isn't solved until the fourth book.

Las Vegas has changed so much, so fast, and so radically since I researched and wrote this book in 1985 that I'm leaving the background "as was" to record what it used to be like. Because of the fast-forward nature of the Las Vegas scene, this is the pattern of the Midnight Louie mystery series too. The characters in the foreground move through a time period of months while the background buildings whiz by, reflecting years of de-construction and construction. It's like the early movies where the actors played a scene in an unmoving car while a montage of background scenes flew by. That's the only sensible way to deal with The City That Won't Stop Reinventing Itself.

And now the Quartet has reinvented itself too. So here it comes again, in a new "authorized" edition.

The credit for the revival goes, in the end, to readers, who live long, and don't forget. In that way, they're a lot like Midnight Louie, the alley cat who wouldn't die.

♦ Midnight Louie Sings the Blues ♦

There is nothing sadder than a singer of sad songs—except a *sad* singer of sad songs, particularly in Las Vegas.

People come to a pumped-up town like Vegas to have fun, and I am no exception to the rule. This town is where I grew up thinking that the siren on a winning slot machine was my mama's lullaby.

Now I am to be seen prowling these mean, manic streets from one in the morning to eleven at night—Tropicana, Flamingo, Sahara (it is no coincidence they are all named after major hotel-casinos)—and I know this: sad faces take the first plane, train, bus, or taxi out of town, depending on how sad they are, which depends in turn on how broke they are.

These days, the Crystal Phoenix Hotel and Casino is my beat, and I am flirting with my golden years, which is to say I go to bed an hour earlier and rise an hour later. Still, on Vegas time, that means I only get about three hours of shut-eye. It is true that a thread or two of silver have insinuated themselves into the hairs upon my well-furred masculine chest. But what the hell; Harrison Ford is getting a trifle grizzled himself. They still call me Midnight Louie.

And life is pretty cushy these days. I have my red velvet recliner in the dressing room of Miss Darcy McGill Austen, the sweetest hoofer to tap "Dixie" in this town. I have visiting privileges in the hotel manager's office, where Miss Van von Rhine will often neglect her managerial and marital duties to slip me a tender tidbit or two from her tea tray. I can be found lounging by the big pool out back, or

9

contemplating the odds near the koi pond. I am a frequent but discreet visitor to Chef Sing Song's kitchens.

In fact, I am discreet six ways from Sunday and all the way into Tuesday. I am blessed with the softest step of any private house dick on the Strip and have foiled dastardly thugs attempting dastardly deeds on more than one occasion, although you never see my name in a newspaper column or my puss pictured in *True Detective*.

However, it is not on my particular feats of derring-do that I wish to discourse. I am by nature a modest dude; now nature seems to be reciprocating by giving me reason for such sentiments.

No, it is the slender white line, whisker-thin, between glad and sad that I am minded to ruminate upon. This subject comes to my attention one evening when I am checking backstage at the Crystal Curtain, which is the in-house theater at my favorite hostelry. (Did I ever tell you how I single-handedly saved the Crystal Phoenix from more than utter destruction at the hands of crazed killers? Perhaps I did.)

Suffice it to say that the Crystal Phoenix is the classiest joint in Vegas, not the largest but the best. The owner, Mr. Nicky Fontana, will have it no other way. And what Mr. Nicky Fontana wants, he gets—an example of which axiom is the aforementioned Miss Van von Rhine, now the gentleman's spouse. I, of course, had a little something to do with that successful experiment in holy matrimony.

Nowadays, it seems like all of Vegas and half the people who visit it—around a million a month—are queued up in the Crystal Phoenix lobby trying to wind their way into the Crystal Curtain Music Theater to hear Gentleman Johnny Diamond sing his sad heart and soul out.

Like all things in the Phoenix, including Miss Van von

Rhine, the Crystal Curtain comes in a small but strictly classy package. A mere five hundred fortunate souls (and yours truly) can squeeze in nightly.

This fact only makes Gentleman Johnny Diamond more popular, a phenomenon of human nature that has not been missed by certain Madison Avenue hucksters. So Gentleman Johnny Diamond sings night after night to misty-eyed tourists who pay fifty dollars per head for the privilege of springing leaks in public, and a fine voice he has for a fellow who has never been called upon to improvise in a back alley without benefit of microphone.

(I am a jazz musician myself, if I can be prevailed upon to exercise the old tonsils, and do my best wailing when inspired by the dark of the moon, an attentive ear of the feminine persuasion, and the exciting percussive accompaniment of hurled shoes thumping assorted brick walls.)

Gentleman Johnny is what we of the old school call a "ballad singer"; that is, he can actually carry a tune and possesses a fine, two-plus octave range to cart it around in. Such abilities are more than somewhat old-fashioned, it is true, and not the kind of thing that goes over big on MTV.

But in Las Vegas, where people spend thousands of dollars on old-fashioned vices like gambling, spiritous liquors, and the opposite sex, having a prime set of pipes is an advantage. It is not as if he is in high demand elsewhere, the movies long ago abandoning the hunt for the next Nelson Eddy, although to give Gentleman Johnny credit, he is a better-looking dude than is seen in most movies nowadays. (I would give you twenty-to-one on Errol Flynn over Dustin Hoffman any day, even as Boy Tootsie.)

So there is Gentleman Johnny in the baby-pink spotlight six nights a week (he gets Tuesdays off), warbling "If Ever I Would Leave You" and "Younger than Springtime" and other showpiece songs from an era when words were understandable and singers were either one sex or the other and weren't trying to confuse their audiences and each other, not to mention their own mothers.

Gentleman Johnny is definitely of the old school, that is to say, what used to be called a heartthrob. (Okay, okay! I go back a long way.) The ladies line up to throw gardenias, roomkeys, and diamond rings at his feet when he finishes his set with "You Made Me Love You."

That is why I hang around every night: you never know when the stage crew might neglect to snag some choice bauble. Not that I am dishonest. It is simply that there is much to be said for "finders keepers," the least of which is a healthy finder's fee. But one night some joker infiltrates the lovesick ladies and heaves a pineapple—not the pineapple of the *Beverly Hills Diet* fame, but the undersized little fellow of WWII fame, otherwise known as a hand grenade—at Gentleman Johnny Diamond's parting bootheels.

It is not a lethal pineapple, seeing as how a twist of paper instead of a pin stuffs it shut, but the paper reads like this: "SING THE LAST ONE FOR ME. A FAN."

That does it. No more freebie listening posts backstage for Midnight Louie. Security is tighter than an airport slot machine. And Gentleman Johnny Diamond's songs get sadder, and the stagehands sweep up the offered loot with padded gloves and a metal detector.

It sort of takes all the fun out of it, and most of that missing fun is coming right out of the star attraction himself. When he croons "Melancholy Baby," he means it. He is now, you might say, just a baritone in a crystal cage.

But everybody is afraid something is going to happen to Gentleman Johnny, who is a fine fellow upon whom you would wish no more ill fortune than the draw of the queen of spades in a game of hearts. And indeed something does happen, but not what anyone thinks.

◆ Chapter One ◆

"This nut may not get to me in person, but I'll guarantee he's going to drive me crazy long-distance."

Johnny Diamond threw the threatening note onto the makeup table's harmless clutter. Its crazy-quilt lettering, cut from a Babel of magazines, reflected gibberish in the mirror.

The man and woman sharing Johnny's luxuriously appointed dressing room exchanged quick glances. Noticing that, he smiled, exposing teeth portals pearly enough to make St. Peter homesick—the capped porcelain splendor of the professional performer.

"How do you know it's a 'he'?" the woman, a natural blonde, asked uneasily.

Johnny shrugged. "He's threatening to do me in, or seems to be. That's not the kind of mayhem my female correspondents propose."

"No way," agreed the other man, rolling sympathetic dark eyes at Johnny's watching ones in the mirror.

The woman's eyes narrowed to mock-suspicion, Siamese-cat-blue slits as she studied her husband. "How do you know, Nicky Fontana, what Johnny's fan mail says?"

Nicky shrugged disarmingly. "Hey, it's my job! I own this joint, don't I, even if you manage it? I gotta read the fan mail to know what my star performer has to put up with." He grinned at her. "You should see what those nice blue-rinsed, white-haired ladies from Iowa put into anonymous notes they throw on a stage. Hot stuff."

"And harmless," she answered. "This"—she picked up

the latest threatening note, or the copy of it the police had let them keep—"is different. It reeks of threat. Perhaps the show doesn't have to go on. Johnny could lay low for a while. The Crystal Phoenix doesn't need to keep packing them in at any cost."

Nicky, a nearly black-haired man whose smile dueled Johnny's in the mirror for dazzling white perfection, raised expressive eyebrows. *Maybe,* they suggested silently, *the little woman is right.*

Johnny sighed, tucking a hand towel around the neck of his open ruffle-front shirt. His onstage person evoked a carefully orchestrated river boat gambler image subtler than Wayne Newton's "rhinestone dude" ensembles.

With his long legs and arms, solid singer's torso, and thick mane of strawberry-blond hair, Johnny Diamond looked heroic in stark, formal black, a black string tie at his throat and black embroidery edging the ruffles at his wrists and down his white shirtfront.

He conjured a half-dozen romantic stereotypes when the spotlights brought his erect figure to life: gambler, dandy, preacher man, thief (if the articles of theft in question happened to be female affections). The only person who didn't buy the Johnny Diamond image even a little bit was Johnny himself, who'd been born John Leonard Dimond in Hicksville, Ohio.

He began roughly wiping the pancake makeup from his face and throat. "No, I'll stay and sing for my supper. The police claim it's the only way to catch this phantom head case. God knows their undercover corps is watching me. And if they aren't, your minions are."

"You mean Fontana Inc.?" Van's fond smile turned wry. They all knew what Johnny meant.

Nicky had been born the youngest of ten brothers. To-

15

gether with their macho Uncle Mario Fontana, they comprised a formidable Family of Las Vegas wheelers, dealers, and sometimes, stealers.

Nicky, however, prided himself on being the white sheep of the Family. He kept his nose and the Crystal Phoenix's books scrupulously clean. That didn't keep the darker sheep of the Fontana Family from regarding him and his as beneficiaries of their special protective services.

"You have an obscene number of brothers, Nicky, you do know that?" Johnny complained. "And every last one of them has been breathing down my neck in turn, like he was my personal guardian angel, only these angels run in a pack! This poison-pen guy hasn't got a prayer of doing a hit on me."

Van propped her chin on his shoulder, her serious triangle of face catlike in the mirror.

"That's the way it should be. We don't want to lose you, Johnny."

"No way, Van." He patted the hand she rested on his arm, then threw the towel with its orange smudges of pancake onto the tabletop. "It looks like I could warble my lungs out at the Phoenix for the next three decades, and nobody'd complain."

"Not us!" Nicky stretched his shirt-sleeved arms wide and yawned politely. "We know a winning ticket when we see it." He glanced at his watch, then at his wife. "One-thirty A.M. Time to hit the sack, Van."

"You see what happens when you get married?" Van told Johnny, laughing. "Romance goes out the window."

"I'm a man of action, not words," Nicky said, getting up. "Look, Johnny, if my brothers are getting on your nerves, I mean, I know there are nine of 'em, but I treat 'em all like . . ."

"Don't tell me. Like brothers." Johnny grinned. "Look, it's not your brothers, Nicky, or even this poison-pen correspondent. It's the way I'm tied down before and after the show. It's bad enough living out of a hotel suite—"

"Hey, we do it too," Nicky interjected. "And this is the Crystal Phoenix, the best little hotel in Vegas."

"No offense, Nicky, but the Phoenix is your home. You've got a wife to share your penthouse, and half the people who work for you are pals." Johnny stood, too, towering six-feet-five thanks to the elevating heels of black back-cut boa Western boots. "Even if the guy doesn't kill me, I'll die of boredom, knocking around my suite with my overeager keepers guarding the door. So you see? He gets to me either way."

"It's true." The smallest frown etched Van's porcelain-smooth forehead. "You're virtually a prisoner in the hotel."

"It's worst after the shows," Johnny admitted. "My energy is still at stage-power, but there's not a damn thing to do. At least before this lethal heckler showed up, I could wander the casino and lose some of my princely salary back to the management."

"That's okay." Nicky smiled expansively. "We don't need your money so bad that we'd turn you loose for any nut case to take potshots at." He pulled Van against his side as he thought, his face absorbing some of her worry.

Despite their vast physical differences—Nicky dark and energized, Van light and delicate as lace candy—the couple struck Johnny as two of a kind, as kin in some deeper-than-surface way. It made him feel more marooned than ever, inside the bright prison cell of a spotlight gel or out of it.

"Don't you two worry." His hand lightly tapped Van's shoulder. She was the soul of the enterprise; Nicky the heart. "I'll survive. And when they catch this guy, they

17

should sentence him to life, listening to every last one of my albums."

"That's too good for him," Nicky objected from the doorway. "What do you think I have taped into the speakers around my rooftop spa?"

"*You* have taped?" Van sounded indignant. "It was my idea."

"I didn't know you were a fan," Johnny teased.

"She's crazy about your albums," Nicky confided. "Wants to play 'em all over the penthouse—upstairs, downstairs, in my lady's chamber. Particularly in my lady's chamber."

"Nicky." Van's fist lightly punched his forearm. "That's priv—"

"—show business," Johnny put in. "It's nice that I'm replacing Montovani. Mere punk rockers'll never make hard-bitten lady hotel managers blush."

Van reddened more and hauled Nicky out of the dressing room. Two alert figures—tall, dark, and the semi-spitting image of Nicky—flanked the hallway door like leashed Dobermans.

◆ ◆ ◆

Van looked beyond them, worried. Framed inside the open door, Johnny Diamond looked almost as good as he did on stage, a tall, lordly, yet loose-knit man whose unfurled voice could wheedle or command the baby spots down from the artificial sky of the theater—a born balladeer who could coax the audience's heart into its throat and its soul into their communal gaze.

At one o'clock in the morning after his last show, he looked a little tired and a lot lonely.

"What'll we do?" Van leaned on Nicky's arm as they ambled down the long backstage hallway. "It does seem rather unfair to Johnny. He's stuck with us."

"It's better than being on the road in your thirties. And what else can he do? Vegas is the balladeer's last stand. It's no accident all those old-time musical comedy stars land on a Strip headliner sign and park there like there's no tomorrow. Where else is a traditional act going to rake in the crowds? People come here to listen to songs where they can understand the words and not have their eardrums shattered by screaming guitars and high-volume synthesizers. It's the last bastion of romance, and Johnny was born to sell romance."

"It's a pity he can't buy a little of it for himself."

"You can't buy romance, Van, any more than I could buy class." Nicky stopped to tilt her chin up. "You got to get it the old-fashioned way. You got to earn it. You know that." He kissed her in ready view of the two Fontana brothers far down the hall who greeted this touching sign of marital devotion with catcalls.

"We've got to do something," Van insisted the moment their lips parted, long after the fraternal hooters had tired of their crude jollity. "Something that'll keep Johnny safe but at least give him more to think about than a crazy fan on his trail."

Nicky sighed. "I'll bounce it around with the boys. Maybe we can come up with something. But don't worry, Vanilla, baby," he crooned in seductive Johnny Diamond style. "You're no fun at all when you worry. Remember the immortal words, 'Tomorrow is another day.' "

"But that story," Van reminded him, "had a very unromantic ending."

◆ ◆ ◆

"Tomorrow" hit Las Vegas as it did every day, with a

sudden, sand-sizzling sunrise that warmed the city for twelve bright hours, then faded on cue into evening to permit the showgirl of American metropolises to put on the neon glitz for another twelve hours.

On the Mojave Desert surrounding Las Vegas, the white-hot summer sun slipped away almost unnoticed in a welter of crimson, looking like a cue ball that had suffered a poke in the eye with a sharp stick, bloodied, and fallen off the green, rumpled-felt edge of the earth.

Eightball O'Rourke shifted a wad of Red Man chewing tobacco to his left cheek and spat expertly at an unwise whiptail lizard that had not yet found shelter for the night. Hit mid-torso, the lizard darted into the dusk, its tail waving indignantly.

"Grampa!" Jill remonstrated, pausing in checking the Jeep's saddlebags.

"Varmits," her grandfather excused himself. " 'Sides, spit never hurt no one."

"—never hurt anyone," she corrected automatically. "Encyclopedia would raise the rooftop if he heard you using double negatives like that."

"Encyclopedia is worse than some church-going female for coming down on a fellow's ifs, ands, or buts. He was only supposed to mind *your* p's and q's, not herd the whole pack of us into grammar school."

Jill sloshed water around in the canteens to reassure herself they were almost full, then unlocked the rifle box on the Jeep's floor to ensure the weapon was properly loaded.

"That's what happens," she noted, "when you give someone power, Grampa." She raced through her inventory in the darkening twilight. "He generally takes it further than you'd like."

"Speakin' of goin' further than I'd like"—Eightball

cleared his throat, no easy task with tobacco juice sluicing down his 70-year-old tissues. "I . , . we . . . don't like you drivin' yourself into town—and out—by dark so much lately. There's more'n varmits around these days: city fellers with evil in their minds. I don't think a young filly like yourself knows what goes on in Las Vegas when the lights go on at night."

"Grampa, I'm not a 'young filly,' I'm a grown woman."

Jill sprang lightly into the high seat, the fringe on her buckskin jacket shimmying. Her battered boot pumped the gas pedal before she turned the ignition and the Jeep's venerable motor out-harumphed her grandfather's voice.

"I know how to take care of myself." She hefted the buckskin bag beside her, drawing out the wooden butt of a big black revolver just far enough to show. "Besides, in my profession, you can't crawl into a hole at night like a sun-soaking lizard. Night's when everybody comes out to play. You know that. Hell, Grampa, you taught me that."

"Taught you too much and not enough," he grumbled in the mock-whine of an elderly person who knows he won't get his way with the younger generation. "You think you're pretty tough, Jilly, and maybe you had to be to grow up all by your lonesome way out here in Glory Hole. But city slickers'll move faster'n a whiptail, and it'll take more'n spit to stop 'em."

"Honestly." Jill sighed. "I'll be okay. Aren't I always okay? Who keeps the gang in hardtack and belly-busters? Don't go all soft on me, Grampa. It doesn't become you. But I will be careful."

With that reassurance, the old man stepped back from the Jeep, and she put it into gear. Bucking like a metal bronco, it charged down what masqueraded as a road, a brush-cleared ribbon of rock-spattered desert.

♦ ♦ ♦

Eightball watched the Jeep's square silhouette bobble against the doeskin-pale sunset sky, his eyes watering from wind and strain and simple old age.

Sure she could take care of herself, he thought, spitting contemplatively into the dusk. That was what him and the boys had raised her up to do, take care of herself. A damn pity that she'd ended up having to take care to them too.

Eightball turned and made for the shambling roofs just visible against a clump of indigo bushes. It was dark enough that the kerosene lanterns inside cast a yellow checkerboard of window squares against the twilight.

The boys would have the worn deck of cards out, and the community whiskey bottle, now that Jilly had gone. Eightball salivated at the notion of both diversions. The gang didn't fret as much about her as he did, but then they weren't kin.

What were they? he asked himself, and got an answer, an answer the government liked to get written down on dotted lines if it ever got close enough to corral a fella and make him sign forms. Dependents, that's what they all were—a blamed, useless bunch of dependents. Except for Jilly, who had the most reason to be one.

Eightball spit again, disgustedly, blind, into the dark. He didn't even reap the satisfaction of hearing it splat.

♦ ♦ ♦

Two miles across the desert already, the Jeep chugged over the harsh dunes to the highway, its headlights piercing the now-total darkness.

Looking up through the dust-sprayed windshield, Jill saw a shooting star. Quick! She should make a wish. She remembered Grandma O'Rourke saying wishes hitched rides on shooting stars.

But she couldn't think of a darn thing to wish for, and the star fizzled out, wasted for all eternity.

◆ ◆ ◆

"Help!"

"Johnny, is that you?"

"I guess you can't disguise 'Platinum Tonsils.' " He quoted a recent rave review. "Is your estimable husband there, Van?"

"Nicky?"

"You have another?"

"Sorry. It is . . ."—Van checked the digital clock on the VCR across the bedroom—"two o'clock in the morning."

She lowered the ivory telephone receiver and eyed the penthouse bedroom with mixed feelings. Nicky was there all right, sitting up groggily among the Porthault bedlinens, stark naked.

Van waved her sluggish spouse to the phone. "What's the problem, Johnny? Nicky'll be here in a minute."

The voice that could waft melodically, even over telephone lines, deepened to a thrilling growl. "Fontana, Inc. They've really pulled one this time."

"Where are you?"

"In my suite. What's left of it."

"That does sound . . . dire."

Nicky staggered to the dresser to take the receiver. "Yeah? Yeah, Johnny? Who? My brothers . . . Which ones? Oh. How many? Two? Twins? Yeah. What about the feathers? Still flying, huh? Um, I'll be right down."

Nicky glanced at Van's suspicious face propped sleepily on his bare shoulder. "*We'll* be right down. Yes, I know they're not wearing much! Van's seen naked dames before."

Van's eyes widened awake. "Naked! Nicky, what on earth?"

He covered the mouthpiece. "Semi-naked, that's all." He winked and addressed the receiver again. "I'm gonna let the hotel manager handle it; this doesn't seem like a job for the owner. Van'll fix you right up, Johnny boy."

"Thanks," she said grimly as he hung up. She'd already exchanged her silky Kloss nightgown for a jumpsuit and was cramming bare feet into low-heeled slippers. "What have the pride of the Fontana Family managed to mess up now? And in a mere twenty-four hours on the job? I thought their assignment was to keep Johnny safe and happy."

Nicky grinned as he buckled his trouser belt. "Well, he's safe, anyway. Sort of."

They quickly finished dressing and left the penthouse atop the Crystal Phoenix, now labeled "Floor Fourteen" instead of "Thirteen" at Van's superstitious request.

The private elevator whisked them down to the lobby, where hotel guests thronged like guppies, swallowing drinks on the rocks and milling vacant-eyed to the rhythmic jingle of slot-machine coins.

Transferred to one of the guest elevators, they glided back up to the ninth floor where the hotel's largest suites were located and where Johnny Diamond resided gratis.

A frowning Fontana brother stood guard at the suite's door, his hand tucked Napoleon-like into his breast. Unlike Napoleon, he had a pressing reason for his pose: caressing the sleek butt of a .38-caliber Beretta.

"Forget the heroic stance," Nicky said as he and Van passed through the door. "Sometimes I think you boys couldn't hog-tie a pixie."

Inside the expansive suite, an occasional feather wafted

like an oversize snowflake to the floor. Feathers, as white as liberally drifted Ivory Snow soap, were heaped atop tables and spilled onto the carpet in gentle mounds.

Two sunken pillowcase carcasses lay abandoned on the long, gray leather seating pit. Near them perched two nearly naked ladies, as alike as one feather to the next.

"Welcome to my well-feathered nest," Johnny Diamond bid Nicky and Van, waving congenially from a leather Eames chair that he shared with some stray pinfeathers. "Meet the Haddock girls, April and May, here in all their unhidden glory, courtesy of Nicky's big brother Aldo."

Aldo, chain smoking on the ottoman, rose sheepishly. Or perhaps he rose doveishly, for feathers fluttered off his uneasy shoulders as he moved.

"You said entertain him, Nicky," Aldo wheedled. "The Haddock girls are the hit of Manny's Strip Code Showroom. I thought—"

"That," Nicky said darkly, "was your first mistake." He folded his arms and regarded the Misses Haddock. "Twins?"

They nodded jointly, long made-up faces in odd contrast to long mostly undressed bodies attired in random bits of glitz. And feathers.

"We were born on either side of midnight, April on the thirty-first of, and me on May Day," said one while her clone watched expressionlessly. "See, April's an April baby and I'm a May." She giggled.

Johnny Diamond opened what was left of the Sunday *Review-Journal* and spread it over his face as if he were sleeping.

Van looked at Nicky, who looked at Aldo and then back to the first Miss Haddock.

"So . . . ah, how did these feathers—?"

"Some guys," Twin Two explained with great care, as though addressing the representative of an alien culture, "like a friendly fight between girls, you know? Anyway, Aldo here said we were supposed to liven up Johnny's life."

The tented front section of the *Review-Journal* quaked.

Van was at the phone, efficiently punching numbers. "I'll get Housekeeping to vacuum up those feathers and replace the pillows." Luckily, Las Vegas hotels have an around-the-clock, three-shift staff, or Johnny would be sneezing goose down until tomorrow morning.

"Aldo, you escort the Haddocks to . . . oh, throw them back, wherever you found them! Pay them or whatever you men of the world do when dealing with . . . er, worldly women.

"Nicky, stop snickering into your palm. I know precisely what you're thinking. Call in every Fontana sibling you can round up and make sure that they precipitate no more fiascos of this nature in the future. Housekeeping? Van von Rhine. I need a maid, two feather pillows, and a vacuum cleaner in nine-eighteen immediately. Thank you."

"Precipitate?" Nicky was doubled over now, looking at the mystified Haddock sisters, then bursting into guffaws. "That's right, it's raining in here—raining feathers!"

"We are not amused," Van declaimed in Queen Victoria tones as Aldo escorted the twins to the door.

"We? Speak for yourself." Nicky collapsed on the ottoman and rolled onto the floor.

"We," she repeated severely, "meaning Johnny and me."

Nicky stopped writhing in laughter long enough to glance at his prize performer. Johnny had lifted the papers to glare out from under the fine gray type of the classifieds.

"I appreciate what your brothers tried to do for me, Nicky, but imported hoofers, hookers, or their kissing cousins are hardly going to lower my blood pressure after a show. I already have enough offers from respectable women to satisfy a convention of traveling salesmen."

Johnny gestured to a pizza-size crystal ashtray on the glass-topped coffee table. It overflowed with room keys, a collection of each night's "take," which would be redistributed to the front desk in the morning.

The keys were ritually brought to Johnny's suite like a clattering bouquet, a barometer of his popularity, but any castaway jewelry that hit the stage rested in the hotel safe. In the morning, when post-show ardor had cooled, claimants submitted to careful interrogation before recouping their gems.

"I might as well take one of *these* lonely ladies up on her offer. But I'm not looking for love, and I'm not asking for sex," Johnny said plaintively. "I just want a—" Johnny sat up and ran his fingers through the thick yellow hair at his temples. "I want a change of scene, of stage set. That's it! Just . . . someplace, something . . . maybe, that's different."

"That could be the answer." Van had walked over to stare at the crystal platter full of room keys. "It might even be safer for you in view of this crazy man threatening you."

"What's the answer?" Nicky had risen and was dusting feathers off his navy trousers.

"We could change Johnny's room. Give him a new atmosphere."

"Change it for what?"

She gestured to the winking brass keys. "Pick your number, Johnny. Anything you choose will be a change of scene."

He joined her at the coffee table, towering over the keys. "I don't want a roommate."

"You won't have one, except for your regular bodyguards," she explained. "These guest rooms turn over like nickel chips. As soon as the present occupant checks out from the one you pick, it's yours."

"The note writer can't follow you unless he can outguess pure chance. Plus"—Van's faint eyebrows raised challengingly—"you know you're settling in a room where somebody who loved your act just stayed. Surely, you have some ego. You can change rooms weekly, nightly if you like. Visit the ghosts of your harem of admirers and never meet them face to face."

"What a bizarre idea, Van," Johnny's big hand stretched over the ashtray, lamplight glinting red off the golden hairs dusting his knuckles. "Even a little kinky. I had no idea." His smile quirked, then widened. "Why not? I choose you, contestant number"—Johnny raised a single key out of the melee and read the figures engraved upon the diamond-shaped lucite handle it dangled from—"Seven-thirteen."

"Seven come thirteen," Nicky quipped. "Not bad. For some reason, I think that's a suite too. My brothers won't have to breathe down your neck, then. Van, why are you kicking me?"

"I'm not kicking you, darling. I'm merely attracting your attention. I really think Johnny should draw another key."

"I like this one." Johnny held it up by the notched narrow end. "It's fate. We belong together, seven-thirteen and me."

"But—" Van still seemed speechless. "That's an . . . abandoned suite. It's never been redecorated. It's just as it was forty years ago when the hotel was built."

"Great. I love local color." Johnny was flipping the key like a coin.

Nicky had stopped watching Van as he watched the key and its lucite plaque somersault through the air before

Johnny slapped the winking shape tight into his palm again.

"Van, is that the key I think it is?"

"Yes," she answered grimly.

"How did it get—" Nicky eyed the pile of glinting keys, a tribute to Johnny Diamond's effect upon the women in his audience. "Hey, Johnny," Nicky tried to intercept the diamond plaque in mid-flip. "This key shouldn't have been in there, man."

"So? That makes it all the more interesting. If the room's vacant, I'll move down there tonight." Johnny glanced around the feather-dusted furnishings. "This place is a mess anyway."

Nicky shrugged. Van bit her lip. Johnny Diamond smiled like a kid who's been told a new toy is waiting around the corner.

Finally, Van called the bell captain to send a trolley and bellman to move Johnny's belongings. She and Nicky wandered into the hall while the staff swept into the room to accomplish the relocation.

"That's the suite, isn't it?" Nicky asked quietly. "I'd forgotten about it."

"I hadn't," Van said, pacing. "I never had it redecorated, never rented it out. It hasn't been touched . . . since—"

"Since we chased ghosts in it and found a few of our own, huh?" Nicky's restless fingers pushed Van's loose hair behind her ear. "Is that what bothers you about putting Johnny in there? It's 'our' place?"

"No. What bothers me is that the key shouldn't have been in that pile. Who threw it? Who had it, a key that hasn't been used in, in ten years." She shivered.

"You're so cute when you're superstitious," Nicky whispered in the ear he had bared, wrapping his arms around her.

She shrugged him off. "I'm serious, Nicky! For once in your life, be a little serious too. We ought to warn Johnny!"

"About what? That some weird old geezer named Jersey Joe Jackson lived in that suite since the forties? That he died there years ago, and the joint hasn't been used since? That you used to room next door to it before you vamped the owner and moved topside? That one night you thought you saw somebody going into it, back in the days when the hotel was semi-deserted and all sorts of drifters hung around the place? Johnny's got enough to worry about with these threatening notes. Don't add your superstitions to his load."

"All right! Maybe it's what he needs, a change of scene. Believe me, suite seven-thirteen will give it to him."

◆ ◆ ◆

The fat man from Peoria tapped his little finger on his knuckles when his cards came up bad.

Tex, the car dealership owner from Amarillo, was fidgeting in his chair, but that could have been the submarine-sandwich-size oval of his silver belt buckle digging into his beer belly instead of the pinch of a poor hand.

Danny, the punk kid from eastern New Jersey, just grinned at his cards, loose lower lip working to some beat only he could hear.

Jill studied the lackluster lay of her cards. It was a sucker's hand, tempting enough to lead her right down Lady Luck's one-way street. A four and a six of diamonds, six and eight of clubs, and a five of hearts. A pair of sixes in the hand was worth zilch in the bush, but she did have the long-shot makings of a straight if she tossed one of the sixes.

She discarded the six of diamonds to even out the black-red ratio of her remaining four cards. No reason; she simply preferred balance to imbalance.

"One," Jill ordered Tex, the dealer, while the other men gawked. They never asked for less than two or more than three cards. But they weren't pros, and she was. A pro had to gamble sometimes, and Jill was betting now on one of four sevens in the deck being the next card. The odds against it were longer than the horizon.

The gilt phoenix backing the house cards winked as it flipped Jill's way. She picked it up. A club. The seven.

Jill didn't do anything when the cards fell her way, any more than she did when they came up snake eyes. She waited expressionlessly while the betting made its rounds.

The fat man licked his lips and raised them twenty. Tex matched him. The kid snarled and folded, leaning far back in his chair to wait. Over Jill's shoulder, past the brass-rail fence that kept onlookers at a decent distance, two slick-looking young men loomed over the gathered kibitzers.

Jill fanned her cards face-up to the table's burgundy Ultrasuede surface. There were a hundred little ways of letting customers know they were in the Crystal Phoenix and not just any ordinary hotel. Van von Rhine used them all.

"Straight," Jill announced.

Tex cursed inaudibly, leaning back to blow out his breath and give his belt a break. His hand concealed a paltry pair of fours.

The fat man, and he was really fat; no neck, no waist to belt, no fingers almost, neatly displayed his cards, one by one. An ace of hearts, king of hearts—"from my original hand," he noted—queen of spades, jack of diamonds. The other men hunched hopefully forward. The fat man's ace-high straight looked much more impressive than Jill's.

The last card came up the jack of hearts, not the ten-spot the fat man needed. Despite the pair of jacks, his hand was a loser.

Jill pushed her Western hat back on her head. Everybody took the hat for an affectation in a city full up with affectations, but she simply liked to wear it.

Under it, her hair fell long and dark, parted in the middle and cut every fourth Saturday night by Spuds Lonnigan after chow time. Her pale, makeup-less face made her look like a choirgirl. Employees always carded Jill where liquor was served, and they always were terribly embarrassed when she finally flashed her driver's license.

So the men who came to Las Vegas to play serious poker, the men who chaffed when the tiny young woman in Annie Oakley rig politely asked to join in, didn't know that Jill O'Rourke was the finest female poker player (maybe the best poker player, period) in Las Vegas.

The watching brothers Fontana, on this occasion Rico and Ralph, did know. One of them—which, it was hard to say, but that's how it was with the brothers Fontana: not being able to tell them apart made them much more effective—one stepped in front of Jill as she rose to leave.

"I never knew a poker face could be so pretty," he began with a courtly smile.

"Can it," Jill said, brushing by.

Tweedledee was left staring, but Tweedledum efficiently slid his pale-suited self into her path.

"You don't understand, Miss O'Rourke," the second brother—Ralph, she saw—said. "We, uh, wish to put a proposition to you in your professional capacity."

"My professional capacity is playing poker."

"We know, we know." The first Fontana brother sidled up.

Jill knew what he was, generically speaking. You couldn't spend much time in Las Vegas without seeing or hearing of Fontana Inc. Now she recognized him as Rico.

"What about a private standing game?" Rico was suggesting, his darting brown eyes revealing that the plan was being formulated even as he talked.

"I don't have the stake for that kind of game." Jill preferred to play the hundred-dollar table; tonight she'd taken a ten-dollar seat out of necessity. Even professionals encounter runs of punk luck.

"This would be"—melting dark eye consulted melting dark eye—"a friendly game. For amusement purposes. Low stakes. But—"

"Then why play?" she exploded. "I like to pretend I do this for a living."

"For a fee! A hundred dollars a night, six nights a week. You keep it, win or lose."

"A hundred—? Why six nights?" She frowned and pushed her hat forward, a sign of impatience she'd never exhibit at a card table.

"Our . . . client's only available six nights."

"No dice. It's four A.M. I gotta cash in." She moved past Rico.

"Wait!" Ralph, overeager, snagged a handful of the jacket fringe along her departing elbow.

Jill whirled, jaw set, eyes deadly.

Ralph's fingers unclenched, his palms suddenly clammy. "Look, you don't even have to show up until after one in the morning every, ah, night. There'll be plenty of time to play the public tables first. This deal would be gravy."

"Who is this poker whiz?"

"He's not," Rico swore. "He's just a guy who gets restless. A rich insomniac, see?" Rico winked triumphantly at his brother, truly inspired now. "And a little eccentric, if you know what I mean."

"What you mean is that only the rich can afford to underwrite their eccentricities." Jill folded her arms and stared sightlessly at Rico's middle shirt button, which was at her eye level.

"So no names," Ralph put in. "And one teensy little condition."

"Yeah?" Jill's face looked as if she ate ground nails for breakfast.

"We gotta . . . blindfold you on the way up. I told you the guy was rich! He's a nut for anonymity. Ask Nicky Fontana who owns this joint. He'll vouch for us."

Jill sighed mightily. "I know he will. This had better be legitimate, or I'll sue the pants off you guys, and the world won't cotton to seeing your knobby knees, I promise you."

"No problem, no problem," Rico was murmuring in a voice as soothing as Amaretto.

A brother on either side, they ushered her to the elevator. There they discouraged anyone else from entering by standing shoulder to shoulder in the open doors, then stepped back and hit the Close Door button.

Inside, Ralph whisked a red-silk handkerchief from his cream wool-blend breast pocket.

"This had better be good," Jill threatened, doffing her hat to submit to an airy blindfolding.

Light leaked through, and the comforting weight of the .45 in her buckskin bag tugged at her shoulder. Jill began to picture her unknown flaky benefactor, her mysterious opponent. Tall and cadaverous. Stoop-shouldered and shrewd. Silver-haired and cagey-eyed. Howard Hughes before he really went off the rails into reclusedom and madness. And old; the old suffered from insomnia, as Jill had reason to know.

"This had better be good," she repeated more softly and more ominously.

"Good?" Rico demanded with customary Fontana modesty. He winked at Ralph over Jill's intervening head and hit the button marked 7.

"Hey, this is a Fontana Inc. production. It'll be great!"

◆ Chapter Two ◆

"What's this? What have you two flakes off the old Italian coconut pulled now?"

The voice came deep, mellow, and affectionately annoyed. Jill felt hands tug at her token blindfold. Gauzy red fell away with a silken caress. Jill blinked while the brighter light resolved into a new and alien environment.

The room looked unlike any she'd ever seen, as if the Fontana brothers had wafted her to another planet. Opposite her, looking just as surprised as she felt, stood a totem-tall man. She had at least gotten that part right. The rest of her speculations on the nature of her mysterious partner were wrong. All wrong. Disturbingly wrong. Or maybe the man in front of her was disturbingly right. Jill held her peace and let the Fontana boys do the talking.

"This here's a little brainstorm of ours," Rico was saying. "It just hit us down on the casino floor. Here's your answer to post-midnight entertainment. Her name's—"

"I don't care what her name is," the man interrupted, weariness muting the sudden anger in his voice. "It's almost three o'clock in the morning. How could you guys pull another stupid stunt like this?"

"You don't get it," Ralph was explaining unctuously. "We had something different in mind than Aldo's gig. She's not—"

"I don't care what she's not, and I don't care what she is," the man roared back like a large and irate lion. "Get out and take your hare brains with you. I'll explain it to the"—for the first time that Jill was free to see, his eyes moved to her face—"the lady."

A closing door behind her told Jill that Fontana Inc. had obediently evaporated. That fact alone raised the stranger in her estimation.

The silence held as he paced, his black-clad figure in focus against a bizarre background of chartreuse. She didn't know which to study first: the outre surroundings or the man so unpleased to see her.

The man won the battle for her attention. For one thing, he was moving, and moving well, like a creature that takes unconscious pleasure in it. He reminded Jill of a chance encounter in a narrow mountain canyon she'd hoped to forget.

She was there again in her mind, on the hot desiccated desert floor, lying flat to press her face into the cold clear bounty of a hidden spring at the canyon's bottom. Something, an alteration in the air maybe, made her look up. From the encompassing beige of the surrounding rocks, a form focused into the huge head of a mountain lion, not two body lengths away from her.

Jill had frozen, stunned by the heavy calmness of the head, by the intelligent eyes peering through a veil of slight surprise at this human intrusion on its private watering hole. She could read the flecks of color in the big cat's eyes the way Pitchblende could discern mineral flakes in raw rock—yellow and blue blending to distant green.

The fresh, ineffable scent of water under her nose mingled with the desert's alkaline perfume and a new animal musk in the air. Jill, prone, was meat ripe for rendering. Both she and the lion knew it. But surprise, not hunger, ruled the animal's pale eyes.

Rejecting company, the lordly beast rose on muscular legs, flicked its long tail, and vanished over the rocks. Jill finished drinking, and returned to the Jeep.

The next day, the rifle cradled in the crook of her arm, she had revisited the spring. Massive lion tracks covered her boot imprints, showing that the lion had come back to drink alone after she'd left. But before that, the lion had shadowed her trail, step for step, the entire quarter-mile back to the Jeep.

Transfixed once again by a presence imbued with some of the same aloof lordliness as the lion's, Jill found herself oddly calm. The man paused suddenly, whipped his fists to his hips, and tilted back his tawny-maned head.

"You're a bit young for this line of work, aren't you?"

Jill's shoulders lowered into her own battle stance as she lengthened her neck to make herself as tall as possible. "I'm small. There's a big difference."

His hands spread in concession, the incandescent lamplight striking sparks off the fine golden hairs misting the backs of them. The same gilt aura gleamed at the neck of his open shirtfront. Hair haloed him like gold dust, like the subtle, taken-for-granted coat on a catamount. It was a pleasing phenomenon, at once patently masculine and extremely subtle. He mesmerized her, this wildly self-certain man, and she wondered if he knew that, and, if he did, how he would exploit it.

"Small." His eyes used her self-description as liberty to make their own evaluation. "That you are, half-pint, but old enough to know what you're doing, no doubt."

"I think so," she answered coldly.

He shrugged and turned his broad back on her. Jill almost expected to see a golden tail flick into view.

"I suppose you have your reasons for the way you make a living."

"It's all I can do," she answered. "And I do it well!" she added forcefully.

The indifferent back twisted enough for a gleam of amber-brown eye to assess her again over a shoulder. "Do you? You're no shrinking violet, that's for sure."

"Try me!" she challenged.

Something in his eyes skittered backward, like a whiptail lizard at her grandfather's on-target spit.

"No, thanks." With a big man's disregard for daintiness, he sat on a Queen Anne loveseat upholstered in chartreuse satin. "I have some vices, but that's not one. So far," he added darkly. "You've been brought here on false pretenses. I'll pay for your time, and you can go." He leaned forward to slap a hand to his rear hip.

"I didn't lose that much time," Jill said hastily before he could produce the wallet. "I was done for the night anyway."

"Were you?" His tone was biting. "Nice of you to add me to your workload. How much did they offer to pay you?"

"A hundred dollars." She swallowed. It sounded like an awful lot now, just for playing a few hands of poker.

"That's too little," he said even more sharply. "Never undersell yourself—?" He expected a name.

"Jill," she said. "And don't worry. I don't."

His arms folded. "I bet you need that spunk in your line of work."

"Sometimes," she said cautiously. "Mostly I have to be a good judge of people."

"People? Or men?"

"Mostly men," she admitted.

"How do you judge me?"

Jill put her hands on her hips to look him over. Her surprise was melting into something else, something that came with a defensive taunt in its voice.

"You're rich. Not just wealthy—rich. You've got more

money than you know what to do with, and so you don't know what to do with yourself. You're used to getting your own way with other people, but you don't like them when they do what you want. You're cautious and conservative, but you can flash claws and teeth when you need to. You wear your reactions openly, like a coat of mail. To keep people at a respectful distance. And you're lonely."

His expression shifted into resentful surprise, confirmation of the ready reactions she had just described.

"What are you looking at?" he asked abruptly.

Jill realized that she was staring at his feet.

"Those are . . . nice boots."

He bent to run his palm over the shiny surface, then glanced to the dust-scuffed, time-curdled leather of her child-sized boots. Regret softened his features for a moment as he studied his own footwear again.

"Custom-made, to my order. Back-cut boa uppers, eelskin inlay. Just the way I wanted them," he admitted, confirming part of her analysis. "They cost me more than any boot has a right to and too little for me to remember how much. But you're right. They're beautiful boots. I'd forgotten."

He read her face for another moment, and Jill knew he would see a fleeting twinge of envy in it.

"But they hurt my damned feet after"—he glanced to the mantle top clock—"six hours on a hardwood floor. All that money, and they hurt."

"Hurt the boas and the eels too," she noted wryly.

"Yeah. You better go. Send in one of the boys to get these damn boots off when you leave."

Jill turned, shifting her shoulder bag. Then she turned back. "I'm the best bootjack in Clark County."

"You?" he scoffed. "You may not be as young as you

look, but you're not one hair bigger. You haven't got the strength."

"Try me!" she challenged again, her eyes flaring.

"Okay." He thrust out one leg, the sheen of rich black fabric tightening against his thigh.

Jill straddled his leg, her back to him, and lifted a booted foot in her no-nonsense grip.

"Relax your ankle, put the other foot on my rear, and push like hell when I say to."

"I don't want to hurt you."

"Put your foot on my backside, darn it, or I'll drag you plum off the settee when I yank."

His silence said he didn't believe her, but she felt a tentative boot brush on her lower back.

Jill took his foot in the stranglehold that Eightball had taught her. "Push now. Jumping Gila monsters! Push now! Push!"

Johnny Diamond, for the first time in his life, found himself hesitating when he knew he shouldn't. How had the Fontana boys aced him into another ridiculous mess? Jill's hip-length jacket had risen as she'd bent over his leg, presenting a small, tautly blue-jeaned rear. He could feel a remarkably strong tug building at his ankle but found himself reluctant to shove off with the zest she demanded.

"Push, dammit, you big galoot!" In moments of stress, Jill invariably swore like her grandfather.

Johnny heaved away, expected to see the pertly presented derriére flying halfway across the room. No such thing happened. The boot popped off his foot like cork from a champagne bottle. Jill quickly straddled and lifted his other leg.

"Now push again," she ordered briskly, reminding Johnny of a TV-drama midwife. He grinned and lifted his boot-free foot.

This time a warm stocking foot conformed obediently to the cure of Jill's lower spine. Compliance struck her as more suspicious than rebellions. The warming imprint of his foot awed her with its size, with the power implicit in that size. "Ready?" she asked, suddenly feeling oddly uncertain.

"Almost." The foot seesawed itself into perfect contact with the swell of her lower spine.

Johnny noticed that the denim was authentically worn on the neat backside it covered, and he frowned, but his toes wriggled, luxuriously free, on their living footrest.

"Cut out the tickling and push," she ordered.

He complied with true force this time, taking her at her word at last. Jill was catapulted forward, the boot clasped in her hands. She caught herself (and her breath) before stumbling.

"There." She paired the boots and set them at his feet, straightening to flip back long, raven's wings of hair that had fallen over her face.

He studied her, taking his time. She stood not much over five feet, even wearing Cuban-heeled cowboy boots. Her ensemble was casual Western: jeans so tight you couldn't slip a garter snake down her pant leg, checkered snap-button shirt, fringed buckskin jacket, a dusty beige cowgirl hat she'd dropped to the rug while dealing with his boots.

She bent to retrieve it now, her hair spilling over her face again like dark corn syrup, thick and rich. Strange, Johnny thought, that a hooker wouldn't wear makeup. Maybe some men liked to pretend they were with jail-bait. The thought darkened his vision for a moment. Most hookers he'd seen were pragmatic veterans or high-paid call girls. He prided himself on not needing their services, even when the demands of his career made meeting women in a natural setting almost impossible.

Why had the crazy Fontana boys brought him this waif of a woman, feisty and semi-frayed and more independent than anyone he'd met in years?

"Your getup must be the Crystal Gayle look, is that it?" he finally asked.

"My 'getup' is what I like wearing," she answered shortly. Then faint frown lines tracked her forehead. "What's a 'Crystal Gayle,' anyway? Is it some new fancy room at this hotel? They call everything around here the Crystal something or other." Johnny, astounded by her ignorance of what he took for granted, laughed. "Never mind," he soothed. "I shouldn't have said anything."

She bent to jam her hat on and pick up his boots. "I'll leave 'em outside the door for shining."

"No!"

She paused, puzzled by his bellowed intensity almost as much as he was.

Johnny softened the order with a smile. "Leave them outside, all right. And then come back in."

Her tan-gilded petal of a face tilted on a swanlike neck. Freckles dusted her nose and cheeks like pollen, he noticed, faint as face-powder flecks.

"I'm tired tonight," he explained. "I might want to just talk. You'll still get your hundred dollars."

Pink swam under her freckle dust. "I don't need your charity. I earn my way. And I don't get my money by just . . . talking."

"Then this'll be something new. Come on, stay a while, Jill. You know you're fascinated by—"

She inhaled indignantly.

"—the room."

Jill held the boots to her breast while she considered it. She kept them neatly paired, their soles supported in one palm, her other hand clipping the tops together. The hides would not so much as buff each other against the grain in her meticulous custody.

"Leave the boots outside the door and come back," Johnny repeated patiently.

He didn't know if she would until she straightened in the open door after depositing his boots in the hall, paused, and then swiveled back into the room, shutting the door.

"Good," he said, meaning it. "Make yourself at home." He stood and stretched cramped toes. "I'll go in here and 'slip into something more comfortable.' I think that's the phrase."

Johnny grinned amiably and disappeared into the adjoining bedroom while Jill craned her neck to glimpse its furnishings.

Her breath eased out as the bedroom door closed. She reached into her jacket pocket for the sealed deck of house cards she'd grabbed before coming up. Guess she didn't need them now, she thought a bit forlornly. Cards were like worry beads or a gun to her, soothing and defensive.

Still, a hundred dollars, just because some rich guy was feeling talky . . . There'd been slim pickings at the poker table on a Thursday night, and Wild Blue needed his fuel.

She parked her hat on a small round end table. All the pieces of furniture were eighteenth-century reproductions: Hepplewhite, Duncan Phyfe, that stuff. Jill knew a Queen Anne leg from a chorus girl's. Encyclopedia had seen to that, as he'd seen to most of her schooling.

Still, Jill tried to move quietly in the room so she wouldn't be caught gawking. She'd seen the interiors of most Las Vegas casinos and knew they came gaudy and got worse. Even the Crystal Phoenix, the classiest, had to kowtow to token garish touches, like the crystal lamp base next to her hat. It was crowned with a corset-shaped shade of white silk with racy red lacings. Her forefinger tripped down the ladder of lacings, then withdrew as if burned. Maybe this guy was into something *kinky*. Maybe he got off on talking to lady poker players.

The bedroom door cracked, and she jumped, her fringe jiggling soundlessly.

He was back, wearing a rust-velour sweatshirt that burnished everything she had found tawny and golden about him to a high, elegant polish.

"Sit down, Jill," he said politely. "Don't tell me those boots don't hurt your feet."

"They don't, honest. I've worn 'em all my life."

He looked skeptical. "Not even a baby bootie in your past? You've had a rough life."

Her flush flared again, hot and temperamental. "No, I haven't. I've done fine. You've got to wear boots in the desert, or the rattlers'll get you. And if they don't, the rocknettle will."

"Is that where you live, the desert?"

"Sort of."

"From what I've seen of the desert, there's no 'sort of' about it. It's either-or."

He moved to a mahogany highboy and cracked the upper doors. Jill, behind him, gasped as the mirrored interior flashed open on rows of crystal barware.

"It looks like the inside of a geode," she said, marveling, edging closer. Johnny turned, and she jumped back.

"Hey, don't bolt like a greenhorn on me," he teased in the voice he'd used a couple of years ago to play Frank Butler in *Annie Get Your Gun*. "It's just a bar. A big girl like you must have seen the inside of a bar or two. Want something?"

"Sure," she said defiantly.

"Name it." His hand swept past a lineup of leading-brand liquors.

"Whiskey. Three fingers. Ice if you got it."

He turned back to mix his usual tequila concoction and pour her Jack Daniel's into the heavy-bottomed glass. Ice waited in the silver bucket; everything a man could want was provided fresh after his show by the hotel.

"What's your name, anyway?" she asked over the clink of ice and crystal. "I like to know who I'm drinking with." It was Eightball's line, but this guy'd never know it, she told herself.

Johnny paused. She didn't know who he was. That made everything—her presence here, the oddly sobering attraction of her fabric-worn bottom, her thistle-edged voice—special.

He turned with a show-biz smile, the glass of strong whiskey in hand. "Jack," he said. "Call me Jack."

She squinted suspiciously at his face. "You sure have pretty teeth. Are they natural?"

"No. You sure are a nosy mite."

"Don't condescend to me." She glared up at him over the thick rim of her glass.

"This is a betting town. I bet, I bet I could pick you up by your elbows and hold you there for five minutes and not even feel it."

"You're on!"

He hefted her easily, his hands under her elbows, which were held stiffly to her sides. Lifting her up brought her freckles into focus. They blanketed a straight but snubbed nose. No tweezer had ever touched her naturally arched dark eyebrows, and her first sip of whiskey still dewed her pale lips.

She stared suspiciously into his eyes, which were on her level now. "You didn't say how much you bet."

"You didn't check the time," he retorted.

She stared at him harder, searching for signs of strain. There were none, and his wasn't a poker face, she'd said so herself.

"I . . . can't drink my whiskey. Like this." She could feel it now, the subliminal tremor in his hands, the steady force being exerted to hold her a foot off the floor, to hold her face level with his.

His eyes seemed to see inside her. "Little girls shouldn't ask for such big drinks."

"I'm not little!" She wriggled furiously. If she could have, her boot would have stomped the floor. As it was, they flailed at his shins.

He pulled her closer, into the warm-textured colored and scented velour he wore, into the invisible miasma of his skin and breath. She looked ahead and saw the lion waiting, a bit surprised but very much lord of his turf.

"Wanna bet?" he asked, his eyes and the sunburst of wire-thin wrinkles on his cheekbones laughing, his lips laughing and the finely winged nostrils. Even his unbearably white teeth were grinning.

"Bets are off." She thrashed, seeking control in the lack of it. "Let me down, Jack! Please."

Maybe the "please" worked. Jill had a feeling it was invoking the charm of his name. Jack. A plain name, but she liked it, especially with all the offbeat nicknames she'd grown up around.

"Sorry." He smiled as he returned her to earth. "I got carried away."

"I got carried away." She turned to find an object of conversation. "You were going to tell me about the room."

"Rooms. It's a suite. Not much to tell, except that everything in here dates from when the hotel was built in the forties. It was custom-designed for an eccentric recluse named Jersey Joe Jackson, Van told me. Van's the woman who runs the hotel," he explained.

"I know who Van von Rhine is. I've worked the Phoenix since it opened. It's a first-class place."

She glanced back to find him looking sad again, the way she'd seen him on first entering this room. Jill shrugged and wandered away into the room's queer corners. The whiskey was warming her like an aromatic mesquite fire, burning with a rare relaxing glow. She almost never relaxed.

"This wasn't here way back then?" she asked, pausing in front of the rear-projection TV. Johnny had forgotten that only hours ago Van and Nicky had insisted on adding it to the suite, along with a bank of stereo equipment.

"No." He paused in front of the huge screen. The sound was off but an early-morning black-and-white horror movie was flickering through its clichéd frames.

"This is neat." Jill collapsed cross-legged on the floor atop the carpeting patterned in red cabbage roses and forest-green leaves and watched intently, her hat set beside her.

Johnny hadn't sat on a floor in more than ten years. He plunked down Indian-style next to her, but she hardly noticed. Her intent profile shifted under the reflected TV images.

He seemed to be watching her underwater, and he thought of a frail mermaid who once had visited a mortal man and made herself regret it. Ondine. She wasn't from the world he knew, this Jill, but she wasn't a water baby. She was tough, like the desert she lived on. Maybe that was how she survived in such a tawdry line of work. The idea of her unsnapping that neat row of fake mother-of-pearl snaps over her small but womanly chest, unzipping those faded blue jeans for any man who paid for it, made him want to crush the thick bar glass in his hand like a can of Coors.

She was ignoring him for the first time since she'd entered the room, snared in a technological rapture of the deep, charmed by the subterranean images schooling endlessly on the fuzzy-focused screen.

He lifted his finger and moved it a paper's breadth past the hair curving along her cheek to her shoulder. She didn't turn.

"What are they like?" he asked.

"Who?"

"The men you . . . work with."

Jill's image-rapt face squinched dismissively. "Old. Young. In-between. Fat. Thin. Most of them have money, but they want to buy respect. Most of them are mean when they've got the upper hand and whine when they don't." She glanced his way. "Most of them are more to be pitied than to be despised."

"Where'd you learn a phrase like that?"

"Encyclopedia," she answered easily.

"And what's so fascinating about a grade-B midnight movie that you can't look at me when you answer a question?"

She turned to him again, stung. "It's just that I . . . we don't . . . didn't have TV at home."

"You had an encyclopedia and no TV set? Jill, everyone has TV!"

"Well, we don't." She looked to the screen, but he could tell she wasn't seeing anything on it.

"I'm sorry. I know everyone doesn't have money. Is that why you do what you do? To help out at home?"

Her profile nodded.

His forefinger curled under the V of her chin and turned her face to his while his eyes measured the depths of hers. They looked green, but maybe that was because of the room's color. She looked a little ashamed, and he hated himself for making her think of herself that way.

"Somebody's got to do it," she said quickly, the sentences tripping over each other in their effort to get out the door of her mouth and far away. "Grampa only could work odd jobs for years, and he's got no social security. And the rest, they can't work, either. So—"

"No parents?"

She shook her head. "They died before I could remember them. And Grandma O'Rourke not much later. It happens."

"Oh, Jill . . ." He reached for her, pulled her back against his chest, his arms wrapped around her arms.

Surprised by the lion's sudden pounce, she relaxed for an instant in his warm embrace. The whiskey lulled her; the sound of her name being crooned through her hair into her ear soothed her. She turned her face toward his, her nose brushing the emery-board rasp of his shaven chin. Then she saw his eyes, or thought she did.

Jill wrestled herself to her knees in front of him.

"Are you feeling sorry for me? Don't you dare! Don't you dare, Mr. Rich Man. I can outthink you, outlaugh you, outplay you, outfight you, outlove you any day! I don't need your rich-man's toys, your big TVs, or your Jack Daniel's. Oh, yes, I noticed; only the best for Jack Be Quick. I don't need your hundred dollars."

She was struggling to her feet, not so easy after two ounces of straight whiskey a long eight hours since dinner and that a bowl of chili in a nearby diner.

His big golden hands reached out and snared her,

warming her outsides like the whiskey had her insides. But he didn't try to come close or pull her nearer.

"Jill, I wasn't feeling sorry for you. I was feeling sorry for me."

She thought about it, reading the truth in his face and voice. She was right; he'd make a lousy poker player. It was just as well he was hooked on talking. His hands burned into her sides through the thin shirting, but she let them remain.

The horror movie unreeled, its quick-changing images of monsters reflected on the side of his face.

"What terms did the Fontana boys offer you?" he was asking. The man was questions through and through, she thought grimly.

Jill looked down at the gaudy rug and summoned her coldest poker voice. "One hundred dollars a night, six nights a week."

"Six nights a week! Who do they think I am at one in the morning—Superman?"

"They said you needed . . . wanted diversion. They thought you'd like me."

"I do." His hands tightened on her waist, almost too much, but for some reason, Jill felt that fact would be dangerous to mention.

Their warmth was seeping down into her jeans and up toward her shoulders. Her blood seemed to be pounding in places it had never thought to pound before, but maybe that was because she was half sitting on her heels and her circulation was being cut off. She stirred, and his hands loosened as if told to.

"Come back tomorrow night," he said. "Same terms. We'll talk some more, maybe watch an old movie?"

"But I thought you wanted to—"

He cut her off. "I want to do what I want to do at the moment. Let's not worry about that. No schedule. No transacting business."

He had sat back on his heels opposite her, like a middle-aged lion contemplating a gambol.

"You're a funny man, Jack."

"Yeah. Hilarious." His finger made a phantom trip along the edge of her hair. Jill held her breath until it had passed the last point of possible contact. "What do you say?"

"A hundred dollars?" She tried to sound terribly businesslike. He nodded. "Well, it's not common practice, but sure." She stood up, retrieving the slack lump of her bag. "It's your time and your money."

He winced. "Tomorrow," he repeated. "Tomorrow night, or morning, or whatever you call it. One o'clock. I'll be expecting you."

She looked over her shoulder on the way out the door. He stood in the middle of the room she was eager to see more of, contained as a mountain cat on a rock. He looked even sadder than when she'd first seen him. Maybe, Jill thought, it was all right to take money for simply cheering someone up. Maybe that was another, less obvious way of winning.

She shrugged and slipped out the door, where the brothers Fontana waited with raised blindfold. One stood with his back effectively obscuring the room number while the other lightly tied the long handkerchief corners behind her head.

"Who won?" Ralph asked casually.

Jill thought about it for a moment. "We both did."

"Great. Then we pick you up downstairs tomorrow?"

Tomorrow. The word did more for her on the lips of the man inside the unknown room than it could on a casual Fontana lilt.

"Tomorrow," she agreed in a crisp, emotionless voice and marched confidently down the hall between her guides.

Alone in his suite, Johnny picked up empty glasses and then sat in front of the TV's mindless, soundless winking. At least he'd keep her off the streets for a few hours. Not the hours before, but maybe the hours after.

Maybe rich men couldn't buy love, but they could buy a few hours off from lovelessness.

◆ Midnight Louie: Footpad on the Tail ◆

I happen to be lounging about the seventh floor when I see this little doll with enough fringe on her jacket to play the surrey in *Oklahoma!* being ushered out by a deuce of Fontana brothers.

This alone is not enough to engage my suspicions, but the fact that Rico the Dandy has sacrificed his French silk handkerchief to make a blindfold does. There is nothing a Fontana brother likes better than his snappy dressing, unless it is a plate of Grandma Tinucci-brand pasta.

It is a plate of Grandma Tinucci-brand pasta—an entire factory of it, in fact—that enables Mr. Nicky Fontana to buy and spiff up the Crystal Phoenix in the first place

Grandma Tinucci, being the Fontana brothers' relative on their mother's side, is a dear old doll recently departed who made a mint with a pasta factory in Venice (California, that is) and left it all to Nicky for good works.

Among such good works, hanky-panky of the type I suspect here does not number. So I am relieved when the Fontana brothers relieve the little doll of her blindfold by the time their elevator reaches the main floor. I arrive there first by sprinting down the stairs, a taxing act for one of my years and girth.

Then they peel off a hundred-dollar bill as crisp as Chef Sing Song's most cherished head of romaine and amble away, apparently pleased with themselves, which is nothing new for Fontana brothers.

The little doll—who, with her eyes unveiled and her Western hat perched on the back of her head, I now recognize for Miss Jill O'Rourke, a poker player of lethal proclivities but a little doll nevertheless and therefore my personal charge—begins to wander away also.

I follow. For one thing, the Crystal Phoenix is so crawling with assorted flatfoots and Fontanas since the threats upon Johnny Diamond that there is little for a first-class house detective like myself to do. For another, I do not wish anything untoward to happen to Miss Jill O'Rourke and her new hundred-dollar bill, although the little doll is used to toting mucho bucks and although she is usually more than somewhat able to look out for herself. And, of course, I also follow because I am congenitally curious.

This morning—and it is two-thirty o'clock in the morning, after all—Miss Jill O'Rourke seems not her usual steely-eyed self. She wanders into the casino, stops at the Baccarat Cove to bid good morning to Mr. Solitaire Smith, the night referee in this most high-stakes game, and moves on to the all-night shopping arcade filled with boutiques of a frivolous nature destined to unburden winning players of their weightier cash.

Here she strolls along the blazing shop windows with her nose all but polishing the glass. No one who spends any time watching people coming and going in Las Vegas has ever, within living memory, seen Miss Jill O'Rourke slow to a stroll on those cute little Cuban-heeled cowboy boots of hers.

But now she strolls. What is more, the windows are jammed as close as bad taste will allow with chiffon, marabou, lace, high heels, baubles, furs, fuzzy sweaters, and other sundries of an expensive feminine nature. (These fuzzy sweaters are quite the rage, I understand, being woven of the hair of a type of rabbit called the angora. I am not much for rabbits, but better they than I.)

Anyway, at one of these trinket-strewn window displays, Miss Jill O'Rourke jerks to a stop as if her eyes were struck by the sight of a locket holding her dear, dead mama's portrait. She sits on her heels to study the window, her hat pushed back and her elbows propped on her knees.

Several people stare at this unusual sight, but I see everything in my time and use her concentration as a cover to weave over for a look-see of my own.

Aside from a row of sherbet-colored satin slippers with more of these marabou pom-poms on the toes, the only thing I can figure that she is giving the eye to is this bottle of perfume whose small size alone smells expensive. Although I am not a fellow for artificial scents, I see it is a pretty little bottle of clear crystal molded around perfume golden as honey.

For a stopper, the bottle has a frosted glass likeness of a somewhat-larger-than-I member of the feline family. (In this I cannot question Miss Jill O'Rourke's unquestionably fine taste.)

She unbends suddenly, marches in, and I see her addressing the clerk behind the counter, who shortly thereafter goes to the front window and, sure enough, withdraws the perfume bottle with fingernails long and red enough to make a tiger blush.

Miss Jill O'Rourke hands over the hundred, or eighty-some dollars of it, and in return soon leaves the shop bearing a small hot-pink bag. Once again she stands a bit puzzled, then looks around as if just noticing that she is surrounded by much bigger dolls on long, needle-thin heels with fingernails and eyelashes to match.

She rolls the bag into a tiny ball and slips it into the

buckskin bag hanging from her shoulder as if it were a particularly nasty specimen of desert varmit or something lethal to tote, like the .45. (Not that there is anything illegal in Miss Jill O'Rourke packing a .45. She has a special permit to carry one, being she often wins big sums at the poker table and is an undersized little doll who may be preyed upon by some of this town's less upright citizens.)

One of the biggest questions in this town is not the length of Boss Banana's stretch limo or the composition of Macho Mario Fontana's toupee, or where Ugly Al Fresco plans to muscle in next. The biggest question is what a little doll like Miss Jill O'Rourke, who sometimes sits down with high-stakes players to gamble as much as a thousand dollars a pot, does with all this dough she wins.

Such matters do not trouble Midnight Louie, who prefers to study real anomalies of human behavior at this late stage in his life.

What troubles a philosophical dude such as myself is why such a tough little doll, being she is temporarily tapped out by a bum streak of luck, which can happen to the best—why such a little doll would spent most of her last hundred-dollar bill on a bottle of Jungle Cat perfume.

The curiosity is killing me, but I am told that is an inherited weakness.

♦ Chapter Three ♦

The Jeep bucked over a particularly rough hummock of sagebrush and sand. For a moment, its headlights invisibly probed a star-studded sky. Then they jolted earthward again to light-bleach the usual desertscape of sagebrush and beavertail cactus.

"Drat!" Jill fought the wheel, glancing anxiously to the purse quivering on the seat beside her. She transferred it to her lap, hoping to cushion it from jolts.

At least cash money couldn't break, Jill told herself in the course of royal lecture to herself. She never should have splurged on a piece of expensive fragility. Nothing fragile survived in the desert. Even the dainty desert forget-me-not was a bristly little annual that roared back into bloom as robustly as dandelions each spring.

Sunup still skulked a dark two hours away, and Glory Hole itself was a kind of desert Brigadoon, more meant to be lost than to be found. The tiny settlement lay far enough from Las Vegas for the flashing casino lights to have paled to memory, deep enough in the Spectre Mountain range to hide forever, and had been forgotten long enough to evade notice on any contemporary map. Even in daylight, Jill sometimes lost her bearings on the way home.

Glory Hole was only what Grampa and the gang called it, anyway, one of a string of ghost towns broken off from U.S. Highway 95 as it rambled through Nye County on its way to upstate Nevada and, ultimately, the real Golden West of California. Rhyolite, Rose's Well, Gold Bar, Chloride, Bullfrog, and Mud Spring Station: they were all spectral dots on the map nowadays, empty names holding ruins of wind-scoured wood or crumbling brick.

Glory Hole was different. Oh, it was as ruinous as the rest, but it still held people—Grampa and the "boys." That's what they called themselves; that's what Jill had called them since she had begun toddling Glory Hole's sagebrush-clogged "streets."

The headlights illuminated a more familiar track as she jerked the Jeep into a well-worn set of ruts. In moments, she spotted the floating square of yellow that denoted a window and steered for it.

Only one window lit the ramshackle row of wooden cabins lurching together like drunks in a Salvation Army Christmas choir. Jill scrambled out of the high Jeep seat just as a coyote bayed from a nearby rise. Under a sickle moon, the full desert dark rustled with the stirrings of its night hunters—furred, scaled, and feathered.

Jill hurried inside. Despite her grandfather's fear of "evil city folk," she found herself more unnerved by the last few feet of her journey between Jeep and doorway in the primitive dark.

"That you, Jilly?" a cracking voice asked from the interior brightness.

"It's not 'Raffles,'" she answered matter-of-factly. "What're you sitting up for, Encyclopedia? I thought Spuds had dawn patrol."

"Spuds had too much sour in his mash. He's sleepin' down the line." The old man reading by the single kerosene lantern pushed up his trifocals and nodded in a southerly direction.

Jill glanced at the rough round community table with its informal decoration of splayed and abandoned poker hands, then nodded.

"It looks like the rats will play when the cat's away," she noted. "Who won?"

Encyclopedia chuckled and closed the orange-bound book that had been around as long as Jill could remember. The Devil's Dictionary, the spine declared in silver letters.

"Your Grampa. Eightball never could stand to lose."

Jill picked up the empty whiskey bottle, suddenly recalling the rich amber of Jack Daniel's oiling a heavy crystal glass. The boys drank from jelly jars almost as old as they were. When one broke, Jill was sent to buy a replacement at some gasoline station along Highway 95, but only a single glass at a time.

They lived with as little as they could, all the men Jill had grown up among: Eightball O'Rourke, Wild Blue Pike, Spuds Lonnigan, Cranky Ferguson, and Pitchblende O'Hara. They lived as if they weren't even there, without anybody or anything, except for Wild Blue, so nicknamed for his love affair with an old Piper Cub two-seater that lofted into the blue sky above the mountains when there was money enough for gas in its tank.

They lived in a string of simple one-door, one-window, one-chimney-pipe cabins strung along the foothills of the Spectre Mountains, which in turn were tucked right under the Atomic Energy Commission Testing Site. Anyone who could read knew enough to stay far, far away.

Three of Glory Hole's residents could barely read. Jill and Encyclopedia weren't among them.

"Win much?" he was asking now, pulling a red kerchief from his baggy pant pocket to wipe his corrugated brow as if the lamplight were overheating him.

"Not much." Jill slung her bag atop the table to remove the revolver. Her hand also withdrew a ball of crumpled hot-pink plastic.

"What's that?" Encyclopedia's eyes gleamed squirrel-bright through his trifocals as he focused on the package.

Jill pinkened to match her parcel, then crammed it back into her purse before storing the gun in a cupboard. "Some tourist gewgaw. I kinda liked it.

"Anyway"—her voice grew businesslike, all apology squeezed out of it—"I'll do better next week. Got a commission to poker-sit some dude at the Crystal Phoenix. Doesn't look like much of a card player, though." She frowned in memory.

"That's how you'n Eightball like 'em," Encyclopedia wheezed, rising to jam the kerchief in his back pocket and then sit slowly again.

"I don't like to skin novices," Jill said sharply. "But all the big boys are in Atlantic City or Reno lately. Or maybe they're afraid to play with me anymore. They don't like women players to begin with."

"Pshaw, child. You're not the kind of woman they don't like playing. It's those city girls with curls in their eyelashes and more false appurtenances on themselves than Fool's Gold has iron pyrite. I'm sure they don't even think of you as female anymore," he consoled her.

Jill's glance narrowed to the one that made grown men's blood run glacially slow, even when they were staring a royal flush in the blue-blooded face.

"Maybe I don't either," she said shortly, picking up her bag. She lunged back into the outside darkness and down the line, finally entering the cabin that was hers.

The lantern was right where she kept it by the door, so she could come in at night, strike a farmer's match from the mayonnaise jar, and light it on the spot.

The cabin came wind-tight, its crannies stuffed with newsprint. Once a younger Jill had pulled out some wads of yellowed paper and found a date: January 29, 1938. The last lackadaisical mining attempts in most of Nye County's ghost towns had petered out in the twenties and thirties, Encyclopedia had said. But the first "bust" in Nevada's silver-mining salad days had come in the late eighteen-hundreds, so Jill knew the cabins had been built even before then.

Still, in her narrow wood-frame bunk snuggled under Grandma O'Rourke's woolen quilt, Jill had been warmed since toddlerhood.

A couple curtain scraps festooned the small window. Someone had chained an old iron-rimmed wagon wheel to hang from the ceiling above her bed. As a child, Jill had feared it would drop on her. Sometimes she'd drifted off to sleep dreaming it was a chandelier, a new word mined from Encyclopedia's capacious memory and passed on to her with other useless nuggets of information as part of her wide, eccentric education. Sometimes she had watched the wheel so hard it seemed to brighten, spinning and sparkling until it turned into the dawn.

She'd seen real chandeliers now, enough of them to outshine a thousand dawns. Jill paused in taking off her jacket. She'd never seen a lampshade that wore a corset before, though. A vision of the odd suite at the Crystal Phoenix shimmered in her mind. Everything there was soft, shiny, and colored like signboards for the edge-of-town Las Vegas motels.

Jill pulled a long flannel nightgown over her head before shimmying out of her jeans and underthings; nights got cool on the desert, even in March. It took more effort to wriggle the tight legs off her feet than it had to deboot a city galoot, she thought angrily, wrestling denim hobbles. Hopping one-footed she knocked against the bedside orange crate, dislodging her purse.

"Oh!" Her hands caught it only inches from the floor. Subdued, Jill unwrapped her impulse purchase and conveyed it to the single narrow shelf above the window on which reposed a museum of keepsakes from various high points in her obscure twenty-six years. A Gila-monster skull bleached to the color of ivory satin and a dazzling amethyst geode Pitchblende and she had found by the old mine. Stones chosen for their sunlight sparkle glowed more mellow in the flickering lantern light. Nothing manmade rested on the rough board.

Jill lifted up the perfume bottle like a new offering, then stepped back to examine it.

The bottle's curves shimmered in the wavering flame reflections, its cognac-colored contents mysterious as an elixir—another of her favorite words from Encyclopedia's grab bag. Jill frowned. The lion's-head stopper seemed to shake slightly from left to right as the light danced. She snatched the trinket down, clutching it tightly in her fist.

No, it didn't work there. It didn't work anywhere out here in the desert. Smooth, expensive, breakable things belonged in cities. Should have left it in the shop window, Jill admonished herself. Her fist unclenched as she absently rubbed the glass against the soft seam-free side of her breast, so it wouldn't scratch as she erased her own besmirching fingerprints. She examined it one last time before interring it in pink plastic again. It might not fit in Glory Hole, but it was lovely and expensive, and she would not become the kind of person who took such things carelessly for granted.

Darcy McGill Austen held the perfume bottle pinched between her long forefinger and thumb. She turned it to catch the light from the wire-caged bare theatrical bulbs surrounding her dressing-table mirror.

Jill held her Western hat upside down under Darcy's hand, moving with that casual hand, ready to catch the bottle if it fell.

"It's a handsome bottle. What does the perfume smell like?"

Darcy, a tall, supple woman dressed more in her skin than a costume, leaned back in her bentwood chair. The Crystal Phoenix offered a smaller show than the bigger Strip hotels, but The Queen of Hearts Revue came with all the tried-and-true Las Vegas accouterments, including showgirls like Darcy.

Jill brushed a wing of hair behind her shoulder with one hand as she considered it. "Smell like? I don't know. Didn't ask."

"Silly. You're not supposed to buy perfume without testing it. I'll open it for you."

Jill opened her mouth to protest, but it was too late. Darcy's long false fingernails were expertly untwining the wire-thin gold cord around the bottleneck and picking at the seal.

"So, Jill, how have things been going at the tables?"

"Slow," Jill admitted, reluctantly turning away from the operation in progress to answer the tall brunette woman who'd come over from the battered lockers. "But I've got this, uh, client here at the Phoenix now, so things should pick up."

"Who is this high roller?"

"Don't know. A real coy fella. All I know is his name's Jack, and the Fontana brothers are bowing themselves into next Sunday to grant his every wish, so he must be rich."

Midge, another showgirl, nodded. Nobody in Las Vegas

ever questioned the eccentricities of rich high rollers; they just thanked God and their paychecks for them. She dipped her towering frame to look in the mirror, adjusting the pull of star-spangled tights across long, lean thighs. At eleven o'clock between shows, the chorus line relaxed. "Shouldn't you be playing now?"

"Hmm?" The stopper was slowly rotating free of the frosted crystal neck at Darcy's patient tugging. Jill looked back at Midge. "No. I've got a standing appointment with this guy for one A.M. Look, I hope my coming by isn't bothering you. . . ."

"Bothering us?" Midge's taloned hands tightened on Jill's buckskinned shoulders and shook her reassuringly until the buckskin jacket fringe quavered like Jell-O in an earthquake. Since most Las Vegas chorus girls were nearly six feet tall, Midge loomed over Jill, making her look even more childlike. "Heavens, Jill, you're one of our backstage family, ever since your grandfather used to leave you with me between shows while he played the poker tables upstairs. You and me have been in more hotels than a traveling salesman. You should come by more often."

"Ahhhh!" Darcy eased the stopper free and cocked a skeptical false eyelash at her dressing-room mate. "You babysat Jill? Say, just how many years have you been hoofing, Midge? You must be getting a little long in the leotard."

"I was a babe in arms myself at the time!" Midge said. "Listen, I'm going to join Jo and Trish for a pizza orgy in the Green Room. You two feel free to come along."

"Here." Darcy, remaining seated, held the bottle top by the small glass lion head and nudged the stopper toward Jill's nose.

Jill sniffed it suspiciously from a distance, nose twitching like a rabbit's, then leaned near and inhaled dramatically.

"Well?" Darcy demanded.

Jill shook her head, bewildered. "It smells, I guess. Not as sweet as Western jimson-weed or catclaw, or as fresh as new leather, but I guess it's okay."

Darcy shook her head. "You don't sound like an ex-charge of Midge's. She'd sell her soul for a quarter-ounce of L'Air du Temps. Well, put some on! I'm dying to find out how Jungle Cat mixes with your usual, natural desert-lily scent. Come on, Jill, you don't want to smell like an extra for *Rawhide* forever."

Jill deposited her hat atop Darcy's powder puffs and makeup sponges, then reached for the tiny bottle. "How?" she asked bluntly.

"Oh. Well, you hold the bottle like I did and turn it upside down so you get some perfume on your fingers, and then you . . . dab it on your wrist—or wherever."

"I'll drop it!" Jill stood paralyzed, her fingers clutching the tiny bottle in much the way Darcy would have held a rattlesnake—at arm's length.

"No, you won't." Darcy twisted Jill's hand into the proper motion. "Now just pat your fingers on your wrist."

Jill complied, then looked up, her hazel-green eyes stricken. "What about the other wrist? My fingers won't reach the wrist on the same hand."

"Tip the bottle into the other hand! Honestly, you'd think you'd never worn perfume before. Oh, sorry. I guess you probably haven't. I keep forgetting you live way out on the desert . . . here, let me do it."

Jill perched on the dressing table edge, much relieved, while Darcy shook the bottle expertly and dotted the released liquid behind Jill's ears.

"I can't smell it there," Jill complained, pulling her long

hair forward to inhale experimentally.

Darcy rolled her eyes as she restoppered the bottle. "*You're* not supposed to. Anyway, you can smell your wrists until kingdom come."

Jill was engaged in that very pursuit. She thrust one toward the sleeping black cat that decked the red pillow on Darcy's makeup table like a furred statue.

"Oh, Jill, Louie has revolting taste in scents—he prefers cod-liver oil," Darcy warned as the dozing feline eyes flashed open.

But the cat reacted with a well-considered yawn, and finished by rasping its tongue across Jill's offered wrist.

"I think he likes it. To eat, anyway." Jill licked at her opposite wrist experimentally while Darcy smiled and shook her head.

"So who gave you the perfume?"

"Nobody!" Jill answered quickly.

"Yeah? I've run into Mr. 'Nobody' before," Darcy said in the wise way of an older dorm sister. She patted Jill's blue-jeaned knee.

Despite their similar ages, both being under thirty, and Jill's regular dressing-room presence, there was a world of difference between them, and it all came down to "growing up in Glory Hole."

"I better snag some pizza, or the others will gobble it all," Darcy said, rising. "Want to come?"

Jill shook her head and stopped Darcy by tugging deferentially on the hip swag of her rhinestone G-string.

"Darcy, where else could I put it?"

"Well, in the crook of your elbows, I guess, and behind your knees."

"Behind my knees!" Jill collapsed in laughter, almost rolling atop her hat. "Why would anyone want to do that?"

"And between your breasts."

Jill sobered. "I think I get that one."

"And in the *hollow* of your throat," Darcy declaimed breathily, like a model selling Christmas perfume on television, "if you wish to be truly ir-re-sisss-table."

"I wouldn't be able to smell it there either," Jill argued.

"No, you couldn't," Darcy intoned knowingly. She grabbed Jill's wrist and inhaled, then made a considering face. "Not bad. Listen, I'll see you later."

Jill remained in the empty dressing room, amid curtains of well-organized clutter. Hanging scraps of sequined costumes trembled in ghostly air-vent droughts. On high shelves all around, feather-fountainhead headdresses trembled in anticipation of their onstage turns.

Jill's fingers reached out to run along a red-sequined leotard cut into tongue-of-flame shapes, then, as if burnt, quickly switched to petting Midnight Louie's nobly indifferent head.

"Pretty strange, isn't it?" she asked the cat. "All this glitter and frou-frou." Jill picked up the stoppered perfume bottle and stared into the glassy leonine eyes. Finally she opened it.

She tipped it semi-expertly, paused to study her wet fingertips, then slapped them to her skin as if batting a mosquito.

Her aim was perfect. An invisible daub of scent she couldn't smell cradled itself precisely in the mysterious, haunting, infamous *hollow* of her throat.

◆ ◆ ◆

Sometimes when he sang, Johnny Diamond saw himself the way the audience must. Parapsychologists might call it an out-of-the-body experience. Johnny called it deja vu.

He'd stare into the dark with the spotlights going nova against a black hole of midnight. The soft, vague glimmer of attending faces shifted like whitecaps on a sea.

Then his viewpoint would switch to somewhere high above, and he'd see himself, small as Tom Thumb, moving in the precise circular beam of a follow spot, singing his heart out. He never heard himself at these times, only perceived a lushly orchestrated Muzak blur in his ears.

He saw his tiny pale hands milk the portable mike of all its nuances, saw himself strut the steps choreographed to make necessity look planned. A singer never dared dance too much, or risked losing breath control. A singer never dared stand still too long, or risked boring an audience.

So he moved constantly across the stage floor while stage effects and filmed collages and occasional nomadic choruses unreeled behind him. He moved like a duck in a carnival target booth, through the same motions over and over, against the same ever-changing background, mechanically puppetlike.

Johnny Diamond had seen, long before the anonymous note sender and hand-grenade tosser, that he made a perfect target in the spotlight.

But tonight his sense of self-distance seemed fresher. He saw himself through the eyes of someone who didn't know who he was—and saw that he himself didn't know. He saw his life as an endless chain of certainties. From the time he began singing in small clubs at the age of eighteen, it had all led here, to becoming the house singer at the Crystal Phoenix in Las Vegas, to doing two shows a night six nights a week, to beginning every show with a dramatically pensive "Send in the Clowns" and ending it with "You Made Me Love You."

Far below, the tiny black figure that was himself

launched into that trademark close, right on schedule. In a sense, the poison-pen fan had added a certain bizarre uncertainty to Johnny's life that success couldn't provide.

And so had she, he realized, the unspoiled young woman the Fontana brothers had rousted from God-knows-where and brought to the strange new rooms a whim had made his own.

Life had suddenly switched from dealing him no-nonsense clubs to his trademark diamonds, which even now were etched in glitter all over the stage floor and winked expensively from his fingers. Or was it . . . hearts?

A glittering blizzard of room keys, notes, and rhinestone jewelry blew toward the stage. Johnny found himself on it again, drawing out the final "you-ou-ou-ou" in his patented style.

What if he suddenly switched to "Swannee" as a closer? he wondered. Would the spotlights fall from his jet-dark heavens? Would ticket sales plummet? What if . . . he asked himself, making his many return bows with automatic grace, bobbing from backstage dark to onstage bright until his eyes pinned stars everywhere.

What if she wasn't there tonight?

◆ ◆ ◆

Johnny strode rapidly down the seventh floor hallway, Aldo Fontana skittering in his rear to keep up. His makeup lay behind him on assorted discarded cotton balls; his diamond rings lay in the hotel safe; even his costume had already been exchanged for a jogging suit. Not a single prop or particle of Johnny Diamond, Singer, remained with him, except for his voice.

Van von Rhine had studded the halls of her hotel with European crystal sconces more useful for decoration than illumination. As he neared the rooms numbered in the seven-twenties, Johnny saw a waiting trio take shape in his spotlight-dazzled eyes. Two tall men and one tiny woman. He felt a stab of anticipation.

"Do you have to use that thing?" he demanded of Rico as he eyed Jill's bright red-silk blindfold. The melodrama of the blindfold annoyed him.

Suited shoulders shrugged with unconstructed grace. "Security."

The sound of Johnny's voice had made Jill jump, although she must have heard oncoming footsteps and assumed whose they'd be. Johnny hesitated before putting a hand in the small of her back, then said, "I'll take it off inside."

He guided Jill in, and he had been right; she had stiffened at his touch. She wore the same jacket, the same boots, the same jeans, for all he knew. Only the shirt was a different pattern, but it closed with the same fake mother-of-pearl snaps.

"You must pick your clothes from the same closet every day," he noted, unknotting the tightly drawn silk at the back of her head. The blindfold fell away to uncover alert yellow-green-brown eyes, sometimes called hazel by the unobservant.

"So must you," she retorted, bristling. Her cabin held nothing so conventional as a "closet."

"Routine is soothing to the soul," he answered as she eyed his jogging suit, this one a navy shade that matched his darker mood tonight.

"And to the pocketbook."

"I thought you said you did all right."

"I do." She was looking around again, ignoring him almost deliberately. "But some times are . . . slow, that's all."

She spun to face him, then pulled something out of her pocket. "I thought I might as well find out what kind of a card player you are."

Amusement lifted his melancholy. "Playing cards? You always carry them?"

"Always," she said grimly. "Along with other things. You never know."

Her changeable eyes were opaque now; he'd call them hardwood hazel if he had to. Johnny shook his head ruefully. The Fontana brothers had sent him a quirky hooker, and she wanted to play cards as if he were a favorite uncle babysitting a tomboy niece.

Johnny smiled suddenly. It might be kind of fun at that. He hadn't "played" anything except a piano in years.

"What do you want to play," he inquired genially, moving to the inlaid card table behind the chartreuse sofa, "old maid?"

She froze and then put the same ice into her glance. "Are you getting personal, Jack?"

"No, no way," he denied, taken aback. He'd forgotten he told her his name was Jack. He'd forgotten that a young woman old enough to walk the streets might resent being treated like a child. He reached politely for the back of her chair.

"Good," she was saying, smartly pulling out the formal mahogany chair before he could touch it and sitting down. "The last thing you want to do in a game of poker is get personal with the players."

"Oh. I see." Johnny pulled out the chair opposite and sat. "Would it be too personal to ask if you'd like some refreshment?"

"No Jack Daniel's. I don't drink when I play." She tilted the hat back on her head and frowned down at the cards as she ripped off the cellophane.

The naked deck slapped to the bare buffed tabletop.

Johnny waited for enlightenment.

"Cut!" she finally ordered. "It's a fresh deck, but you can never be too careful. That's rule number one."

Johnny cut the cards.

"How much?" she wanted to know next.

"How much what?"

"How much are we playing for?"

"Ah, twenty?"

"Twenty dollars a hand or twenty dollars minimum bet?"

"Which is better?"

"It depends on who wins," Jill said, raising a raven eyebrow. "Since you're a greenhorn, we'd better just make it ten dollars a bet. You look like you could afford to lose twenty dollars every five minutes, and that's about what a hand'll take."

"I'm only too happy to supplement your income in an honest manner, so deal away, Miss O'Rourke."

She glared at him.

"What's the matter now?"

"Are you making fun of me with that 'Miss O'Rourke' stuff?"

"No, of course not, Jill."

She picked up the deck in her small, efficient hands, then paused.

"Is something wrong?"

"Well, I could stand to wet my whistle. My throat's dry for some reason."

He got up and went to bar, pouring them both well-iced ginger ales. When Johnny glanced back at the table, Jill was sitting there stiffly, her hat beside her, watching him.

She sniffed the glass when he brought it to her.

"Ginger ale, straight. I swear," he said. "What's made you so suspicious tonight?"

"We're playing cards," she said promptly. "That's the only way to do it, suspiciously."

The deck opened and closed like a tiny accordion in her hands as she shuffled crisp new cards with awesome speed and skill.

"And speaking of suspicion"—Jill looked Johnny straight in the eyes for the first time that evening—"my hat's on the table."

"I noticed."

"It shouldn't be. I could be hiding extra aces underneath it."

"Then take it off the table," he suggested patiently.

"You can't expect me to tell you everything! It's up to you to offer a challenge."

Johnny sighed. "All right. Would you please, Miss O'Rourke, remove your headgear from the playing surface? This isn't old maid we're playing, you know," he added sternly.

"Teach somebody something, and they turn on you," Jill grumbled, Eightball-style. She'd heard hundreds of his cranky monologues before she'd won her first game of gin rummy from him.

But she moved her hat to the floor and favored Johnny with a spotlight-bright smile. "You're too trusting."

He regarded her oddly. "No, but I think maybe you are."

"I can take care of myself!" she flared, fighting the same old inference with the same old argument.

"Maybe," he conceded with the beginnings of a poker face. "Maybe it'd be more fun not to."

She gasped in justifiable outrage but had no ready answer. Instead, she did what she did best. She dealt the cards.

"This is seven-card stud," she began instructively, "and I'll thank you not to snicker. There's nothing funny about poker except not taking it seriously."

An hour and a half later, a stack of ten-dollar bills lay in front of Jill. Their last hands lay face-up on the fine-grained wood, and Johnny was rubbing his neck.

"How'd you do that?" He stared at the piled money in front of her, less with regret than perplexity.

Jill grinned and swept the bills into her hands. "We can lower the bets tomorrow. Say, a dollar a round?"

"Are you kidding? Even I know that the one-to-three-dollar poker tables downstairs are a joke! I can afford to lose . . ."

". . . two-hundred-and-sixty-five, seventy, seventy-five, eighty," Jill finished counting. "And that's with time out to explain fine points. Playing poker with you, Jack, is like taking quarters from the tooth fairy."

"I'm new at this," he answered smoothly.

She turned her face sideways the better to squint skeptically at him. "You're taking this awfully well. Doesn't it bother you, losing all that money to a *woman?* To a *little* woman? Heck, doesn't just plain losing bother you?"

Johnny smiled to himself and rolled the melted ice cubes around in the diluted ginger ale in his glass. "Well, you're a woman, I think." His quick confirming glance made her glower. "And you're little." He looked her over again. "And I lost, all right. And none of that bothers me. Does it bother you?"

"Yes, it bothers me! Hellation, what's the use of me winning if you don't want to win too?"

Jill scooped her hat up from the floor, tucked the bills into an inner elastic hatband, and dragged her purse atop the table with a rather resounding noise.

"You carry your money in your hat?"

"You bet. Keeps my hands free."

"Free for what?" He seemed disbelieving.

Jill pulled the .45 from her soft-flapped purse and aimed it at the wallpaper.

"My God!" Johnny drew back. A six-inch revolver barrel looked like a cannon in the double grasp of Jill's small hands. "You don't carry that thing regularly?"

"I do."

"Put it away."

"Why? It won't fire unless I pull the trigger."

"I know it must be dangerous at night for people who are . . . in your line of work, but—"

"It's dangerous anytime for people in my line of work," Jill said matter-of-factly. "And I know how to use this thing, and not use it. I could puncture that piece of ersatz bamboo right in its knobby knee joint if I wanted to."

She raised the weapon to the wallpaper again and sighted along the dull black barrel.

"No!" Johnny's hand turned the barrel, unerringly steady, aside.

"Hey, don't get fingerprints on it! I just cleaned it." Jill, miffed, put her weapon in her purse.

"Who taught you how to shoot?"

"Pitchblende."

"Pitchblende?"

"He was a sharpshooter in the Rangers in WWTwo." She said "double-u, double-u two," like the vets do.

"But *Pitchblende?*"

"That's just what *we* call him. I guess the army had another name for him. He's a friend of my grandfather's."

She pushed back from the table with the professional card player's indifference, now that the dealing was done.

"You were going to tell me more about the room. I've never seen curtains like that, not even in the dining room of the Goliath Hotel."

Johnny joined her in studying the elaborately arranged silver-gray satin draperies at the windows.

"Have you ever seen pictures of Betty Grable in one of those World War Two upsweep hair-dos?" he asked.

"Sure." Jill nodded eagerly, recognizing common ground. "Wild Blue's got a calendar chock-full of girls in seamed stockings and not much else. He kept it since the war."

"These curtains are that old. That's why the top swags resemble forties hair styles."

"Oh." Jill, awed, lifted her head to gaze at the sculpted satin swirl of fabric on valance.

Behind her, Johnny swept the tilting hat off her head.

She rounded on him like an enraged terrier. "Give that back!"

But he was holding it above his head. Even without the exaggerated heels of cowboy boots on his feet, that was far too high for her to reach.

She jumped for it anyway, bounding up against him as if he were a navy-velour tree trunk.

"Settle down!" he ordered, laughing. "I just wanted to see how high you came without your hat on."

"How high I came where?"

"On me."

"I wouldn't be on you if you didn't have my hat!" she retorted.

"But I do, and you are," he answered reasonably, his lion-yellow eyes laughing down at her.

Jill took account of herself, every muscle straining as she stretched against him for the high teasing target of her hat.

She backed off, chin lifting.

"Just hold still a minute, and the worst'll be over," he urged, stepping forward again.

They stood toe to toe, and the tip of her nose brushed the velour of his jogging shirt. His hand pressed the top of her head, then drew a line at his breastbone. The velour's soft nap held the mark.

"There." He put both hands on her arms to set her back, then paused. "Now I know how high you are, but—"

"But what?" Exasperated as she was by his teasing, Jill was even more intrigued by his next gambit. It was as if Jack were playing a kind of poker hand he knew much better than she, and winning.

"You—please don't take this in the wrong way, Miss O'Rourke—but you . . . smell . . . different tonight."

She began nervously brushing her hair forward over her shoulders and face. "It, um, could be pollen. Desert pollen. Cactus is blooming this time of year."

"No." Johnny frowned, lowering his genial golden face to hers. He sniffed with a connoisseur's persnickety nicety. "It smells more expensive than that. It smells like some fancy perfume—"

"No! You couldn't smell that, not perfume!"

Jill's dark hair was a shimmying sheet of denial. She tried to shrink away from him, somehow not quite managing it.

Johnny drew closer, bending to regard her face. Her hair shook more wildly. Even Jill could sense the rich, hoarded odor of Jungle Cat fanning from the warmth behind her ears.

Embarrassment only fueled the fire. Johnny's face, so close that the faint zephyr of his breath stole across her features one by one, dipped below her chin.

"Eureka! This is the culprit spot, this is . . ."

Jill's world tilted at an unsustainable angle as she leaned away from him. His hands held her fixed for his too-close inspection.

Mortified, she lowered her shoulders, raised her head and prepared to confess to the odiferous presence of perfume. Her defiant posture wasn't lost on Johnny. This bizarre mingling of expensive scent and untrammeled nature made him feel sudden tenderness for a woman ashamed of one small fragrant vanity.

"All right!" Jill clenched her teeth, ready to admit all.

Before she could, she was arrested by the sight of lamplight sheening the man's lowered mane of blond hair. She thought herself paralyzed before a desert spring again, surprised by a creature as surprised as herself. Both so surprised. . . .

The man lowered his face to drink as if this spring were his territory and she was the intruder in her own body. His lips moved to her skin and pressed warmly on the infamous, irresistible, expensively perfumed hollow of her throat.

◆ Chapter Four ◆

Jill grabbed her hat back from Johnny's nerveless fingers. "Why'd you do that?" she demanded.

Johnny blinked. Her eyes looked as cool and green as water in this light, he noticed, but her slightly sandpapered voice was hotly indignant.

"I don't know."

"Oh." Jill folded her arms across her chest, sleeve fringe swaying, the retrieved hat hanging from one hand. "First, first you, you go and smooch a person, and then you claim ignorance."

"I guess I like you."

"Do you kiss everybody you like?"

"No." His eyes sharpened in amusement. "Usually they're girls."

"I'm not a girl! I'm a woman and a poker player! I'm the best darn woman poker player in this town! Men don't kiss me." Her pride revised the assertion. "There."

He was frowning at her in a slow, easy way that made her realize she liked the expression on his face as well as any other and that she hadn't seen any yet that she didn't like.

"Poker player?" he was asking slowly, as if he wanted to get it absolutely straight. "A poker player—that's what you are?"

The hat hit the floor, and so did a size-five boy's boot heel, emphatically.

"Of course I'm a poker player! Why the hell else would I be here, dealing perfectly decent cards to a dude who wouldn't know what to do with a cinch hand if it jumped up and tap danced on the table? And then you go and, and—oh!"

She whipped around, showing him her back.

Johnny studied the fringe sashaying wildly along her shoulder blades until it almost hypnotized him.

"Jill, I'm sorry. I mean, I'm not really sorry." The buckskin-clad shoulders heaved. "I thought because the Fontanas dug you up and brought you here that you were—But you're a *poker* player? I thought you were a hooker," he blurted.

She whirled to face him, anger arming her better than stainless steel. "And that's why you kissed me on the neck? You thought I was a hooker?"

"Yes! I mean—no! I'm sorry. I thought you were a pro, yes. Some quirky, amazing street girl. I was never going to—" He saw the morass awaiting any man about to disavow dishonorable intentions toward any woman and backed off. "But that's not why I kissed you."

She was backing off, too, toward the door. Johnny inserted himself between it and her. She could leave, he realized, just leave and never come back, simply because she didn't want to. The money wouldn't be enough to hold her. It had never been enough.

She pulled up short, her arms still folded so tightly across her chest, it took him a moment to remember that she had a most satisfactory one.

"Then why did you?" Jill asked reluctantly. She didn't pout; she was far too forthright to pout. "Why did you kiss me there?"

Johnny could be forthright too.

"Because . . . that's all I've ever seen of you, besides your face and hands," he said earnestly. "And your face is always telling me that you mean business and to back off, and your hands are always dealing cards or packing pistols. That little triangle of skin that's hidden by the shadow of your hair before your shirt closes down on it is the only piece of you I've seen that's soft and sweet. And you did plant some perfume there—"

"I am not sweet!" Jill raged, pacing. "Ask any player on the Strip. Any house lookout man. They'll tell you Jill O'Rourke's got hot hands and icicle eyes. She is ruthless. She plays like a man. She doesn't have one sweet bone in her body! What're you trying to do, Jack, ruin my reputation?"

"I just said I thought you were a hooker, and now I know you're not. Your reputation was ruined before I met you."

"Only with you! And that was your mistake. I guess thinking there was any way to earn easy money was mine! Here!" Jill bent, picked up her hat, and tore the wad of ten-dollar bills from its elastic lodging. "I don't need your money! You're a lousy poker player, anyway. And besides, you kissed me *before* you knew I wasn't a hooker, so . . . so what does that make you?"

Ten-dollar bills fluttered unheeded to the cabbage-rose carpeting. Johnny caught a departing Jill by the crook of her arm, whirling her back into the room as if she were his partner in a do-si-do.

"That makes me a guy who likes a girl, no matter how she makes her living, okay?"

Her eyes grew ice-green. "I told you: I'm a woman, not a girl. Can't you learn anything?"

"Maybe I need a patient teacher."

"You don't need anything I know. You don't care about poker! You just thought I was some hooker with an interesting angle. You pays your money and you gets to see the funny woman take herself seriously."

"Jill, no." His voice had softened as hers had hardened. Johnny saw her eyes looked like ice only because they glittered with tears. Angry tears, he qualified quickly. Righteous, woman-size tears. "You can say anything you want about me. I *am* rich. I *am* spoiled. But don't underestimate yourself, Jill. I kissed you because I care for you, that's all. If that offends you, I'm sorry."

They both paused, struck by his sincerity, Johnny because he'd been pouring the technique of sincerity into songs for fifteen years and the real McCoy came out sounding false, Jill because she was an impeccable judge of faces.

She looked at Jack's now—still frowning with worry—and abandoned the smokescreen of her own emotional brush fire. Jill shook her arm free of his hand, a loose grip easy to dislodge at that, and settled down her shoulders.

"You're not completely hopeless," she conceded.

He looked confused.

"At poker," she elaborated. "I guess I could stay and teach you a thing or two."

"What about . . . other things?"

"It's not supposed to work." Jill looked steadfastly at the floor between their feet. "That's just the lies they put in the magazines, that it actually works."

"What's not supposed to work?"

She kept her head down. "I wouldn't have put it on if I had known it really works." She looked up, her cheeks pinked with honesty. "I didn't mean to make you do it, honest, Jack."

He studied the dark crown of her head while she contemplated the carpeting again, then bent to bring his face nearer hers.

He spoke as softly as he could, which after all those years onstage, wasn't easy.

"What if I kissed you someplace where you hadn't put it? Then you'd know you hadn't cheated."

She looked up, amazed that he had understood so well.

His face was very close as he wrapped his arms around her and lifted her up with him. Paralyzed, Jill wrapped her legs around his hips, her arms around his neck. His face moved nearer, instant by instant. "Oh," Jill said, realizing only then what he'd intended.

A kiss as deliberate and warm as a desert wind ironed itself to her lips.

Encyclopedia had a fancy French phrase for it—fait accompli. Already done. It was already done. Or already begun. By saying "oh" she had merely parted her lips to the continental divide of his.

Jill's stomach lurched as it did when the Jeep jolted over the top of a ridge and down again. She was suddenly aware of being off the ground, out of control, of someone dealing cards wearing faces she'd never seen before, of one-eyed jacks carrying Cupid's bows and winking queens caroming in some endless shuffle in her mind.

Jack, she thought. What a lovely name. Jack, she thought again. Jack . . . of hearts.

◆ ◆ ◆

"So you take care of them now—the boys—with your poker winnings?"

Jill bristled. "It's only fair. They were stuck with me for so long when I was just a kid and didn't contribute anything."

"How old are these Lost Boys?"

"Oh, Grampa's seventy-five, and the rest are around that, I guess. I never asked. How come you are? And why do you call them lost boys?"

"I'm surprised Encyclopedia didn't make sure you read Peter Pan. He seems to have overseen your education pretty thoroughly." Jack tucked a strand of her hair, which he had previously delighted in pulling loose and twirling around his fingertip, behind her ear.

They were curled up together on the chartreuse-satin Queen Anne sofa, or rather Jill was curled up against Jack while he leaned back with his feet up on the plump seat cushion.

"So who were the lost boys?" she prodded.

"Just that. Boys who vanished when young to some Never-Never Land where they could play at all the things that enchanted them forever. Your grandfather's crew sounds like that."

Jill shrugged, a motion that wormed her closer into the comfortable groove between Jack's arm and torso. Her feet hadn't touched ground, quite literally, since Jack had picked her up to kiss her.

First he had carried her to the sofa where he had concentrated on getting her boots off. That done, he had sat beside her, leaned back, and pulled her atop him so matter-of-factly, she really couldn't muster a reasonable objection.

Now Jill's toes wriggled in the thin boy's-size socks she always wore inside her cowboy boots. She curled her blunt-nailed fingers into the thick folds of Jack's velour shirt. The fabric folds lay slack, like a great cat's skin. Jill's eyes drifted half shut. Jack had become inextricably blended with the mountain lion she'd encountered in the desert, yet it was she who curved into him, limpid as a kitten, and who kneaded her satisfaction into his chest. Jill felt sleepy, safe, and completely wonderful.

She yawned. "I guess they're lost boys at that. Wild Blue's always dashing up yonder in his Piper Cub on some wild goose chase for the Last Camel."

"The last camel? Is that a cigarette or what?" Jack's deep rumbling voice sounded as lazy as Jill felt.

"No, it's just that Wild Blue has had this obsession since he came home from the War."

"That's 'WWTwo,'" Jack clarified.

"Of course." Jill stared at him as if it were daft to consider any other military conflict since then "the war."

"Anyway," she went on, "the U.S. Cavalry tried using camels out here in the nineteenth century, only the experiment failed, and the camels went wild. Most of them died, but people kept reporting seeing camels—oh, way into the thirties and forties. Wild Blue's convinced that there's one camel descendent still out there, he claims he's seen it, and he flies and flies looking for it. Says it'll make his fortune to find the Last Camel. He's a little tetched."

"And you buy his gasoline with aces and eights."

Jill tensed suddenly. "That's a 'dead man's hand,' Jack. The one Wild Bill Hickock held when they shot him. I play to lose any ace-eight full houses I see developing." She frowned and wrinkled her nose, finally scratching it unconsciously against his chest. "Maybe we humor Wild Blue, but he is a sweet old fellow. They all are.

"Encyclopedia's the most learned man west of the Pecos since Judge Roy Bean, I swear, and he learned it all himself. Pitchblende, he's looking for a still-rich mine somewhere out there on the Mojave. And when he isn't, he does the prettiest watercolor sunsets you've ever seen. Spuds Lonnigan makes the best sweet-potato pie in Nye County, when we can get 'em. The sweet potatoes."

"And your grandfather's the brains of the operation?"

"I hate to brag, but he could euchre Doc Holliday by bucking a pair of aces with a duo of deuces. He's the best."

"Then why isn't he in the casinos playing for your suppers and paying for Wild Blue's fuel bill?"

Jill half sat up, disturbed. Their sudden separation allowed a wedge of room-cooled air to expand between them.

"Eightball's the best! He taught me everything I know. I played cards with him since I was four years old—go fish, rummy, hearts, poker, old maid."

"Aha!"

She caught the teasing forefinger he was shaking at her in her fist.

"I never could beat him, Jack, never. I could beat all the others, but not Eightball. And then one day—I must have been about sixteen—I beat him. I beat him with a crummy two pair, nines and fours, not even face cards! A loser's hand. And I beat Eightball at poker."

Her voice shook. She looked at Johnny as if she expected him to contradict her, as if she were claiming that she'd stopped the sun from rising.

Johnny tried to understand. "You beat him. It had to happen sometime, Jill."

"No! I'd never done it before. I tried and tried, and I wanted to so bad, since I was ten I had wanted to. I swore I would someday. I didn't like losing all the time. But then I won, I really won! And I was sorry."

"How did your grandfather take it?"

Jill shrugged and looked down at her neat, card-clipped fingernails where they lay fanned on the navy velour covering his chest.

"He seemed . . . glad. He held up my hand and yelled 'Champion.' All the boys came in and clucked over the cards and smiled. And I—"

His hands covered hers just as they spasmed into fists.

"I smiled and they brought out the whiskey bottle and

gave me my first straight shot and we all congratulated each other. Afterwards, I went back to my cabin. I ran back to my cabin. And I cried."

"Jill," he said softly. "You didn't mean to win."

"But I did! I did more than anything!" Her eyes shone wildcat fierce. "I just didn't know how bad winning could make you feel."

Johnny sighed deeply. Jill rode the easy rise-and-fall of his powerful singer's chest with a passenger's complacency. She had finally accepted that she could be no burden to him.

"Losing's worse," he said shortly.

"Maybe. I won almost every time after that, against Eightball. It was like some pattern had been broken, and once broken, we couldn't put it back the old way. He couldn't win, and I couldn't lose."

"As soon as I got legal age, I went to the casinos. And I won there, too, but I never had a very big stake and had to play the lower tables. So I made money enough to keep us and keep Wild Blue flying, but never much more than that. Sometimes, though, I'd run across a greenhorn." She smiled suddenly, blending freckles with dimples.

"And you'd fleece him!" Johnny finished, pulling her against him again.

"I like you," she said suddenly and bluntly, making his emotions regroup again. "I'll teach you poker, and maybe someday you'll beat me."

"Maybe." He doubted it. "But I don't want to, Jill."

"Then why play?"

"To pass time pleasantly. To get to know you better. To convince you to trust me."

"Why should I trust you?"

His forefinger pressed the mother-of-pearl doorbell of

her top shirt button. "So we both can win the game I have in mind."

"Can we?" Her eyes grew colder. "Can we both win that kind of game?"

Johnny changed the subject. "I know you've been dealt some lean cards, living in the desert all your life with a poker hand of five old men. Have you ever come out of that shell long enough to have a boyfriend?"

She turned as scarlet as the queen of hearts. "None of your business!"

His forefinger slid behind her shirt placket and popped the first snap loose. Jill gasped as if she were going under water and confessed.

"I had a couple, one really, once."

"And?" Jack's finger popped the next snap loose.

"And . . . he was nice," she mumbled. "A college dropout traveling Highway 95, doing whatever got him money, watching people, seeing country that nobody saw."

Jack pulled the next snap loose without comment. Jill glanced down. Jack's finger had hooked itself in the narrow bridge of bra fabric between her breasts. It felt warm and natural there.

Jill felt unnaturally warm everywhere else. As she stirred, Jack's finger ran along the edge of her bra's Lily of France shimmer. Las Vegas chorus ladies had advised Jill on matters feminine since childhood. Her underwear was as fragile as her outerwear was sturdy and practical.

Jack was realizing that; the grin on his face told her so.

"And?" he asked again, popping the last snap before the stiff waistband of her jeans intervened.

There was no use pretending anything to a man who could look down your open shirtfront, Jill figured.

"He left to fight forest fires in Oregon finally. That's

what he did; followed fires and volunteered. He wanted to save something."

"Did he make love to you?"

"Yes, but not like this."

Jack's eyes widened in surprise. "I'm hardly making love to you yet."

Her fist hit his shoulder softly. Her eyes were dead serious. "Don't bluff me, Jack. I know a man who holds all the cards when I see him."

"I've kept you up all night," he said, turning his head to read the mantel clock.

"It's not morning," she argued.

"It is," he said more calmly than he had a right to, than any man had a right to under the circumstances. "You'd better get your cards together and head home."

Jill reared back in disbelief, her lazy, dreaming mood shattered. She had never known a man who would fold a hand as sure as the one Jack held when he held her.

◆ ◆ ◆

The Jeep was waiting in an almost empty parking lot. A new shift of hotel workers came on at seven A.M., but by then, most serious gamblers had moved on to breakfast elsewhere or a quick sleep in some crash pad.

Jill rarely saw her Jeep in the city's bright daylight. She always came and went to and from Las Vegas in darkness, like a thief. She'd had the vintage surplus vehicle Pitchblende had found for her painted powder blue, a whim that now struck her as a frivolous, empty gesture into the plain face of the life she'd always lived.

Catapulting herself into the seat, she turned on the ignition. It started with the same rough throb as always, the seat thrumming beneath her. This morning that raw vibration shook her emotions as well as her body. She leaned her head back and closed her eyes in the shade of the ragtop.

Damn Jack! How could he do this to her? Rev her motor like that and send her on her way solo and unsatisfied.

Jill shivered as a memory whipped like summer lightning through her innards. The jolt was cleaner than a shot of the South Dakota Everclear hundred-and-fifty-proof alcohol Wild Blue sometimes brought back from his secret hops in the Piper Cub.

Everclear Jack. Jill grinned both defeat and triumph at the nickname. *All right, Jack,* she told herself—and him—as she shifted into gear. *This Jeep can't run on pure alcohol. Let's see how far you and I can go on pure frustration. While you're being so noble and trying not to take advantage of me, maybe I can draw the winning cards in this little one-on-one poker hand of ours.*

♦ Chapter Five ♦

Lunch was a catered affair.

Johnny usually relished lunching with Van and Nicky on their rooftop deck. The view wasn't much, only the blurred pastel pink and blue of distant mountains, but he enjoyed the couple's company, their byplay that was half business and half marital repartee.

Today the lunch hour came too soon after a sleepless dawn. He'd hated to see Jill go but could find no honorable reason to keep her. Johnny winced at his powerlessness as he lifted his hand to shade his sleep-cheated eyes from the overhead sun.

"Tired?" Van always played the perfect hostess. "We should have canceled our lunch. Maybe the performance schedule is getting to you. You must be worried about this mad fan on some deep level."

"Worried, hell." Nicky undid an intricately folded napkin with one flick of the wrist. A knowing grin overlay the genial warmth of his Mediterranean features. "Ralph and Rico tell me that they've finally found Johnny the right midnight distraction. Kept him up almost till sunrise today, I hear."

"Sunrise? Ralph and Rico?" Van's cool demeanor heated up ten degrees. "Nicky Fontana, what have your brothers done now?"

"Imported a professional poker player for the edification and entertainment of our star attraction. I hear Johnny's become a regular card sharp."

"Hardly," said the card sharp in question, sitting politely back in his chair while a Chinese waiter wafted a delicate

92

broth floating one paper-thin carrot slice to the table. "But it does take my mind off . . . other things."

"Who's the pro?" Van asked absently, one eye on the service. When special guests called at the Crystal Phoenix penthouse, they were treated like royalty.

Before Johnny could answer, Nicky crowed the news. "Jill O'Rourke! She gets a regular play fee, plus all she can skin off our novice poker ace here."

"Better watch out," Van warned. "Jill may dress like a rodeo railbird, but she's lethal with a deck of cards."

"I've noticed," Johnny answered. "It hasn't been too bad, really. I've only dropped a few hundred." He sipped the exquisite Oriental subtlety of his soup. "So she's well known around town."

"How could anyone miss her?" Nicky wanted to know. "With all the glitz in Las Vegas, some dame in denim and buckskins is gonna stand out a mile, even if she is only four feet tall."

"Five feet even," Johnny corrected.

Across the table, Van's pale eyebrows lilted politely. "How do you know so exactly?" she inquired.

"One learns things from poker partners, you know," he said. "Maybe not the lay of their cards, but other things."

"If you learn anything from Jill O'Rourke, let me know," Nicky interrupted. "That's one mysterious lady. I remember when she was underage and couldn't play, she used to join the railbirds along the big-stakes poker-playing areas, just watching. Always watching. The first time she sat down to play it was at the Goliath—the Phoenix wasn't renovated then. They tried to have her ejected, first for age, and then sex. 'We don't want no lady at our table' is how the boys put it."

"Really!" Van frowned. "I hope the hotel management

set those chauvinists straight."

"No, ma'am," Nicky said, deadpan. "But Jill O'Rourke did. She pulls out this Colt .45 that is almost as big as she is and sets it on the table.

" 'You don't have to worry about a thing, boys,' she says, cool as last night's coffee. 'For one thing, I'm not a lady, and for another, you won't have enough money left to underwrite a trip to the pay toilet when I'm through with you.' Naturally, they can't boot her out and let it look like they're afraid to play her. She cleaned them out too. Every last one. I love that girl!"

"She's a woman," Johnny corrected absently. This time a raven-black eyebrow lifted questioningly. Johnny shrugged. "I heard it from the lady herself, and she's not one to argue with."

"That's for sure." Nicky was still chuckling as the waiter presented an oval platter of duckling and shrimp, Szechwan style. "That gun's come in handy, though. Once some guy took her size at face value, followed her out after she'd won, and tried to mug her in the parking lot."

Johnny grew still as rock while Van sat forward, her pastel features paling even more. "Mug her?" she demanded. "I didn't know that."

Nicky nodded. "So he waits in the parking lot and grabs for her hat, where she stashes the dough. Jill just goes for the revolver in her shoulder bag. He gets a bullet crease in his sleeve and she gets to keep the money. What a girl!"

"Woman." Van corrected him this time, her bright blue eyes fixed on the seriousness of Johnny's. "It's not funny, Nicky. I've seen Jill come and go ever since I got here. One takes her for granted, after a while. But she's in a dangerous profession. Isn't there anybody to take care of her?"

"Yeah, but I think *she* takes care of *them*," Johnny said

ruefully. He pounced on Nicky. "Since you know so much about Jill, what's the story? She says she lives in the desert with her grandfather and his cohorts."

"The Spectre Mountain Gang," Nicky confirmed.

"Gang?" Van's voice went up a half-octave.

"Don't get antsy, Van. They're just a harmless bunch of old coots. Desert rats. Jill's folks died in a car wreck or something. She was just a baby, so her Grandparents took her in, only Grandma died a couple years later. Grampa skedaddled with Jill to the desert, where his old pals hung out."

"Maybe we should be alarmed." Johnny pushed away a half-full plate. "Do you mean to tell me nobody noticed that Jill grew up without going to school, with no friends her own age, and with a pack of over-aged jokers to support?"

"Hey, everybody takes care of Jill!" Nicky shook his head affectionately. "The hoofers, the security people. Even our new baccarat referee Solitaire Smith tips her off to high bettors and usually he doesn't volunteer nothing to nobody. Why'd you think Rico and Ralph corralled her for you? They saw lean pickings at the casino poker tables, so they steered her to a fatter turkey—you!"

"And killed two birds with one stone, huh?"

"Exactly! They did okay that time, didn't they?"

"Yes, they did okay." Johnny's sudden, thousand-watt smile showcased his teeth.

Van and Nicky relaxed again without knowing why, although Johnny did. You didn't discard stage presence like a London Fog raincoat. It was always with you, an invisible cloak of confidence that people got used to feeling, if not seeing. He knew how to use it to avoid facing the offstage music.

"How is the meal, honored guest?" asked a small man in a three-piece pinstriped suit who had materialized on the redwood decking.

"Superb," Johnny admitted, "but I'm afraid I didn't do it justice. You're the chef?"

"Mr. Sing Song, head chef for the Crystal Phoenix," Van presented the Asian man. "He used to prepare it all himself, but now his children"—she nodded at the young serving man—"are old enough to do the major work. Thank you, Chang."

"Sing is executive chef now," the older man said, smiling. "That means I watch and they work."

"So Sing can sit out behind the hotel tending the koi pool," Nicky threw in. "Rare goldfish are a hobby of his."

"And he goes to English language classes now," Van added.

"You're doing very well," Johnny complimented him.

Chef Song bowed modestly and adjusted the fall of his expensive suitcoat. "But when offspring goof off," he confided, "language skills go bye-bye. I understand why Mr. Diamond not eat all off his plate. Many worries," he added confidentially, bending near to personally remove Johnny's dish. "But a full stomach banishes empty thoughts. Okey dokey."

Johnny chewed on the chef's advice after he left. "I guess my threatening fan is common knowledge. At least I've gotten a personalized fortune cookie motto from the chef. I think I'll catch up on my sleep before the show."

Van's hand rested on Johnny's arm as he pushed away from the table. "You're not worried about the threats, are you? Nothing's happened in three weeks."

"No, no. I'm not worried. About the threats."

"He's worried about losing all the dough we pay him to

Jill O'Rourke," Nicky put in, grinning.

"Not that, either. She won't let me wager more than ten bucks a betting round."

"You let that little spitfire push you around?" Nicky sounded incredulous.

"From what you told me, I'd be crazy not to. Anyway, if I play my cards right, I might learn something about that mysterious background of hers."

Nicky walked Johnny to the door. "Fifty bucks you don't learn so much as her birthday."

"I'm not a betting man."

"Aha!"

"—but you're on."

Nicky's jaw dropped. "What makes you think you can find out what all of Las Vegas has gotten used to not knowing?"

"I've got," Johnny said, smiling, "a secret system."

"Jill, sit down."

"Sure, but aren't Spuds's lunchtime hash browns going to curdle?"

"Haven't made 'em yet," Spuds confessed from his traditional position near the venerable wood-burning stove. He walked over, bow-legged beneath his white, time-stained apron, to sit at the big round table on which they ate and played cards.

All the boys were sitting there in the "community" cabin—Jill's grandfather, Pitchblende, Encyclopedia, Wild Blue, and now Spuds.

Jill pulled out a heavy spindle-backed chair and joined them, her eyes as guarded as when she sat down at a casino poker table.

"You fellows look like a convention of crows at a funeral," she commented edgily. "What's up?"

She studied them, the men she took for granted living with and taking care of, the men who'd taken care of her or at least provided for any needs that were apparent. She studied them with Jack's "lost boys" in mind.

They were "boys" only by a massive leap of the imagination. Their heads shone with varying degrees of baldness, their jeans were as worn as hers, and their boots as scuffed. They did dress like boys, she conceded to herself, like boys playing cowboys, only it all came so naturally to them that she couldn't imagine them dressed any other way, just as she couldn't see herself in satin and frills.

"Okay. Put your cards on the table. Who wants to deal?" Jill asked, meeting the five sets of age-paled eyes gathered around the table.

Their eyes all lowered, except for Eightball's.

"Jilly, we been worried damn white about you. Here you've been going off to town night after night, and you've always come back by sunup before this. We decided"—he looked around to net a quartet of silent nods—"we decided maybe you should fold your poker-playing hands for a while. There's a lot of shootings in town these days. It's getting dangerous in civilization."

"Oh, Grampa! The game ran . . . late, that's all. I'm fine."

"But maybe we're not." Pitchblende, a tall, cadaverous man with a mournful mustache, intoned that in his deep baritone like the knell of a passing bell.

"We're getting old, Jilly," Spuds put in. "I kin hardly peel a potato in one long curl like I used to, my hands shake so bad. We can't take worrying about you, maybe 'cause we know we can't go to town and help you, and we wouldn't be much use to anyone anymore, even if we could."

Jill studied Exhibit A, Spuds's age-freckled, extended hands. They shook.

She shrugged. "Who needs potato-curl wigs to play with anymore? Not me! I'm a . . . grown—"

". . . woman," her grandfather finished, sighing. "You are, and maybe you'll want to stay in town permanent some day. There's nothing out here but our crazy will-o'-the-wisps."

"The last camel is not a will-o'-the-wisp!" Wild Blue pounded his leathery fist on the wood. "It's out there. I seen it. Don't you remember, boys? I was flying over the desert low enough to rub shoulders with the yuccas while Encyclopedia took that photograph. And we both saw it, clear as day." Wild Blue's name memorialized his eyes as much as his obsession; nowadays, they were the same soft blue as faded denim.

Encyclopedia hit the table with a flat, flaccid palm. "Hell, Wild Blue, I'm too fat and too creaky to climb into the backseat of the plane with you now. Sure, I saw the camel, and sure we know it's out there, but darn it, what good does that do when we're too weak to do anything about it if we do find it again? And what do we need the money for, after all this time—?"

Every man at the table froze at the mention of money. Eyes consulted one another and avoided Jill's.

"You mean the money that Wild Blue could make with that camel in the circus," Eightball said firmly.

"Right." Encyclopedia suddenly seemed eager to elaborate. "That's the money Wild Blue *might* get if he found that camel. If it isn't, er, dead yet, like the rest of us will soon be," he added sourly.

"Hey, don't scare Jilly. We'll be around." Spuds's gnarled hand squeezed her shoulder.

99

"What is this all about?" she demanded. "Have you guys been drinking all night? I've been doing this for years, and now you get all worried?"

"You've never stayed out all night," her grandfather put in with gravelly reluctance. "We got to thinking it might be because of a reason we've got no call to ask about, 'cause you're right, Jilly. You're all grown up now. Maybe you want to move to town, leave us out here."

"No!" She slammed her hat to the tabletop. "Who'd take care of you?"

"We take care of ourselves, Jilly," Spuds put in softly. "You never cooked or cleaned or sewed."

"Who'll pay for things you need if you get sick? Make sure you get to a doctor? None of you has gone in years, and Pitchblende still limps because of how Spuds set his leg."

"Who takes care of the coyote or the old ringtail cats, Jilly? They get old, and then one day you just don't see 'em around anymore." Her grandfather's voice sounded firmer than she'd heard it in a long time; even firmer than when he'd declared her the poker champion so long ago.

Jill overturned her hat and began pulling out greenbacks. "Look, nearly three hundred again! You can't expect me to quit now, when I've got a mother lode like this to tap. That's why I stayed out all night. I was winning!"

She pounded the fluttering bills to the tabletop.

The boys looked at it, unimpressed.

"Who's this easy mark, anyway?" Encyclopedia wanted to know.

"A man who doesn't care if he loses a little money. This is tip money to him; it's a lot to us."

"What's his name?" Eightball asked

"Uh, Jack."

"Jack what?"

"I . . . don't know!" Jill drove her fingers into the hair at her temples. "He's eccentric. Wants to remain anonymous. But his money is good—cash!"

She lifted a fistful and shook it under their gathered whiskey noses.

"That's just it," said her grandfather. "You shouldn't have to sit up all night playing with men whose names you don't know. It ain't ladylike. Maybe you want to 'retire,' stay in town, get a job, settle down."

"You didn't teach me how to get a job!" Her hands riffled through the money again. "You taught me how to win this." She looked from face to face. "Are you trying to get rid of me?"

The table was quiet enough for a World Series of Poker showdown.

"What Eightball is saying," little Wild Blue Pike put in, his vague eyes roving the cabin ceiling, "is that *you* might want to get rid of *us*."

"No, no!" Jill swore. "That's crazy. Don't worry about me. I know where the door is. I can walk. And, besides, I'm on a real winning streak with this private party I'm playing right now. I don't want to quit."

"We don't want to quit neither," Pitchblende finally contributed. "But we might have no choice about it. Someday, something's liable to hit one of our old tickers right on target."

"We been living out here, chasing dreams so long, it just occurred to us," Eightball said, "when we were sitting up worrying about you not coming . . . back. It occurred to us that maybe we won't never find what we've been squatting here almost forty years, most of us, to find: Wild Blue's camel or Pitchblende's lost mine or his perfect sunset to paint that gets bought for a commemorative postage stamp. It dawned on us that you could waste your life the same way."

"It's not a waste." Jill gathered the ten-dollar bills into neat, deck-like piles.

Her eyes narrowed in an expression the old men had never seen before and that certainly didn't belong on the face of a poker pro. They narrowed dreamily, as if squinting through a distant, desert-dirty window.

"Besides, I don't know what I'm looking for yet, so there's no point sending me somewhere else to not look for it."

Jill pushed back her man-size chair and rapped her fingers impatiently on the table. "That do it? Ground covered? I really could use some sleep."

"Sure, Jilly, sure." Spuds rose quickly. "I'll have a snack ready when you wake up."

She paused at the door on her way out. "Don't worry about me. I can take care of myself. I'm a big girl."

"You've always been a big girl, Jilly," Eightball answered slowly. "Maybe it's time the rest of us grew up, too."

◆ ◆ ◆

"Did your, uh, grandfather's 'gang' worry about you being out all night yesterday?" Johnny asked, fanning his cards tight against his fingers. His big hand kept Jill from glimpsing any cards, now that he'd learned to hold them close.

"Worry? Them?" Jill made a dismissive face. "Naw. They hardly noticed I was gone."

"Is it a long drive?"

"Where?"

"To wherever you live."

"Long, but not too long."

"And where exactly do you live?"

"I can't say, exactly." Jill met his eyes with a discouraging stare.

Jack's yellow eyes looked particularly owlish tonight, she noticed. Perhaps it was the brown velour jogging suit he wore. He seemed to be hibernating inside it, like a bear, big and hunched and closed down for a chilly spell.

"If I didn't know better," Jill announced suddenly, frowning, "I'd say you had the beginnings of a poker face going there."

The face remained inexpressive. "I'll take . . . one," he said.

"One?"

"One."

"One card, whoo-ee! You must be sitting on the lost Silver Slipper mine there, Jack."

His face stayed sober, unrevealing. Jill peeled the top card off the deck and cast it precisely where the heels of his hands rested on the table.

Jack slipped it into his hand, not a face muscle twitching. Jill studied the minuscule lines around his eyes, hoping for a clue to his cards in their tightness or relaxation. Tonight they were granite-steady.

She glanced at her own hand.

A lackluster pair of kings looked back at her. She dealt Jack his one card, then gave herself three.

"Raise you ten." Jack pushed the bill into the center of the table.

Jill had drawn nothing but unrelated low-spot cards. She hazarded her ten anyway. "I guess I gotta pay to see 'em."

"If they're cards, you do."

Jill looked lightning-fast to his face. Jack's expression was blandly self-satisfied, like a big cat's.

"That's what we're playing," she said.

103

"If you say so. See 'em and weep."

He laid the cards down, one by one. Ace of hearts. Ace of spades. He paused to make sure she had registered the pair. Then he laid down an eight of diamonds and an eight of clubs.

She held her breath.

Jack laid down his last card, the ace of diamonds. "I think we in the trade call that a full house."

"Fold." Jill collapsed her cards, then rapped them edgewise on the tabletop.

Jack was grinning from Sunday to Friday, teeth on perfect parade. "How's that? My first full house. My first winning hand against the best little poker player in Las Vegas!"

Jill pulled the cards into an untidy pile, shuffling them back into the deck.

He tweaked her hat brim. "Hey! Don't I get something for winning?"

"You got the money."

"What about a pat on the back? Or, do you hate losing that bad? This isn't a serious game, Jill."

"Yes, it is!" Her eyes lifted from the cards, icy-hot with emotions that even now shuffled through her mind so fast he couldn't read them. "No, I don't like to lose, to anyone. Yes, I'm glad you're doing better. I'm glad I taught you something, but—"

"But what?" Jack's watching whiskey-blond eyes distilled patience; his rum-warm voice poured it on thicker.

Jill threw the cards down on the table, loosing them like a pack of dogs. "You shouldn't have built on aces and eights, Jack! That's—"

"I know. The 'dead man's hand.' You don't believe that superstitious nonsense, Jill?"

"No! But, but . . ."

"Hey, you taught me that playing to win is important. I drew three aces and an eight. What else could I have done?"

"Discarded the eight, gone for a fresh pair."

Johnny began picking up the scattered cards. "What's really bothering you, Jill?"

She spun away from the table, throwing her arm over the chair's top rail and resting her face on the rough buckskin pillow of her sleeve.

He was the last person she could tell what was bothering her, bothering her so much she couldn't even concentrate on poker. So she told him the second most bothersome thing.

"I've been thinking about the Fontana boys outside, and the hardware they're toting. About why I don't know the room number and why I'm always brought here blindfolded." Her head turned over her shoulder. He could see only an unrevealing, cold slice of her face sandwiched by hat brim and buckskin. "Who *are* you, Jack?"

His face remained noncommittal. "I can't say, exactly."

She spun to face him again, her face closed as a fist. "Someone might want to hurt you."

He shrugged careless shoulders. "Maybe, but it's not serious."

"Who?"

He finished gathering the cards and handed her the deck. "A mysterious stranger, with the cards to my heart. Deal." Jill tensed. His eyes were glittering like yellow fool's gold. He was teasing her and warning her off and making love to her all in one look. She didn't know which reading made her more nervous.

"Or don't you play winners?" he inquired gently.

Glaring, Jill snapped the cards to the table. She won the next five hands, playing the odds with computer-like efficiency.

"My last ten," Johnny said, laying a final bill in the center of the table.

"You'll have more by tomorrow night," she told him.

He nodded, yellow hair gleaming as if gold-dusted in the forty-year-old lamplight.

Aces and eights danced into the back of her mind. "Maybe you won't be here."

"I'll be here."

"Then maybe I won't be."

He sat more still than the moon at midnight. Jill stared into his newborn poker face, then spun away again, cushioning her head on her arm, biting her hand to keep an irrational little whimper from escaping her throat.

She heard the chair creak, felt him come and stand over her. Hands encompassed her shoulders and lifted her to her feet.

"Maybe we've been playing too much poker," Johnny crooned comfortingly. "Maybe you should go home, wherever that is."

"I love poker!" Jill insisted numbly.

At the door he leaned down to flick her hair back over her shoulder and whisper in one ear. "Jill, I'm sorry I won."

"I can lose!" she said. "I have before."

His eyes grew mountain-lion wise. "Not to me."

She thought he was going to kiss her, and waited. But he didn't. His hand paused on the doorknob.

"Come back tomorrow?"

She sighed, publicly. "I'll come back. I'll come back with bells on!"

Her fringe danced angrily down the hall as Ralph led her, blindfolded, to the elevator.

Johnny's restraining hand kept Rico by his side for a minute.

"Follow her," Johnny said softly. "Find out where she lives."

"Follow her? You must be crazy, man! It's three A.M. and she knows that desert like a sidewinder. Besides, she'd plug anybody who tried to tail her. Give me a break. Giuseppe is coming on and I was gonna get some sleep."

Johnny patted Rico's well-tailored back. "Thanks a lot. You're a pal." He winked.

Rico, bedazzled by the Johnny Diamond spell, found himself trailing his brother to the first floor and Jill to the parking lot.

Dawn found his mired Camaro wheels spitting sand up at the car's spotless finish far out on the desert, with the bouncing blue dot of a Jeep vanishing into endless, monotonous distance.

♦ ♦ ♦

"Well?" Johnny turned from his own freshly scrubbed image in the dressing room mirror to face Rico at the door. The show had unwound like satin ribbon tonight, and he was thinking of ordering a bottle of champagne for his room.

Rico, his eyes ringed in fatigued plum shadows, fidgeted. "You followed her?"

"Until dawn did us part."

"And where does she live?"

"Northwest," Rico said authoritatively. "Somewhere."

"You couldn't tell?"

"It's all desert, Johnny! The Camaro gave out on Highway 95 on my way back. It's gonna be in the garage for a week."

"You couldn't keep up with one lone, small woman? What kind of a hood are you?"

"I'm not a hood," Rico corrected pridefully. "I'm a, a gentleman of persuasive instincts."

"Couldn't you have persuaded your car to keep up?"

"With a Jeep? Those things are built for rock-bottom roads."

"A Jeep?" Johnny sat back to contemplate another piece added to the puzzle of Jill O'Rourke. "She'd look kind of cute in a Jeep."

"Real cute," muttered Rico, who been confronted with the news of a complete suspension job at eight A.M. that morning. "A baby-blue Jeep."

"Baby-blue . . ." Johnny's speculative baritone made the color sound like a Bing Crosby phrasing.

"If it'd been puce and purple, I couldn't have kept up, Johnny! What I needed was a half-track. It's wild country out there, nothing but sky and brush and mountains and ghost towns."

"Maybe she's a mirage, Rico. Have you considered that?"

"You don't seem too mad about this," Rico commented cautiously.

Johnny threw down his makeup towel. "Why should I be mad? I'd hoped you could solve some questions about the mysterious Miss O'Rourke, but I'll just have to interrogate her myself. Tonight."

He turned back to tidy up the dressing table, whistling.

Rico cleared his throat.

"Yes?"

"About tonight." Johnny was all ears and eyes. "I saw her in the lobby, as usual, and—"

"And?"

"She's not coming." Rico pulled something from his pocket. "She said . . . give you this."

Johnny's waiting fingers were ice-cold by the time Rico

placed the small piece of pasteboard between them.

The card bore the picture of a pensive yellow-haired man staring sideways into the distance. It was the Jack of diamonds.

◆ Chapter Six ◆

Jill leaned her elbows on the chrome and brass rail separating the upscale baccarat playing area from the rest of the Crystal Phoenix casino.

At one in the morning, only a handful of players sat at the tables discreetly scattered under the moneyed radiance of Austrian crystal chandeliers.

House referees, notable for their black-tie formality, chatted together. A chestnut-haired man in a burgundy-velvet evening jacket spotted Jill and came to the railing.

"I'm looking for a man," she told him quietly.

With anyone but her, the remark would have triggered a flip retort. With anyone but him, she would have gotten one.

"Gambler?" He spoke so discreetly that his taut lips hardly seemed to move.

"Not . . . really." Jill sighed and looked away momentarily. "A rich man."

"You know where he hangs his homburg?" The man's slight Aussie accent lent a humorous twist to his words that his deadpan expression didn't.

"Here." When the man's eyebrows rose, she shrugged. "I know where he is. I don't know what he is. Or who. I figured you see everything that goes down in the Phoenix, Solitaire."

"I see all and sometimes know all, but never tell all," he admitted, narrowing bottle-green eyes. "What are the parameters?"

"Big. A big man. Blond. Early thirties. Good hands.

Western boots. A voice you wouldn't forget."

Solitaire began to shake his noncommital head.

"He might be in the mob," Jill admitted.

"Blond?" He sounded incredulous.

"I think someone's after him."

A small, slow smile blurred Solitaire's razor-lipped expression. "From the way you described him, Jill love, I'd wager half the chorus line at the Stardust is after him."

Jill twisted away from the rail, her face tightening. Solitaire's hand, white lightning with the cards, caught her wrist to delay her.

"Sorry. He must be important."

"He is."

He thought again, then released her. "I don't have a guess, offhand. But I'll work on it."

"Thanks. You're a pal." Her hand brushed the burgundy-velvet sleeve in mute thanks.

"We play the same game, don't we?" he noted. "Only you play your solitaire in a crowd. It's the least one loner can do for another." His fingers rose in a farewell salute.

Jill rushed through the jammed casino, oblivious to the calculated percussion of coins pouring into slot-machine bellies. By the elevators, the crowds dissolved into insignificance as one large single-minded figure bore down on her, the man in question.

"Jack!"

Behind him, breathless, rushed two Fontana watchdogs.

He waved the jack of diamonds in her face. "What do you mean by this?"

"Whatever you think it means. It's my calling card."

"But you're not calling tonight. Jill, what's wrong?"

Passing Las Vegas tourists ignored them. Livelier shows inside the hotel theaters outdrew any intimate emotional displays in the lobbies. Las Vegas habituees were used to seeing fortunes lost and hearts broken in public. A few discreet feet away the Fontana boys shuffled sharkskin shoes. Elevator gongs rang out in random rhythm.

"Nothing," she told him reluctantly. "I can't play tonight, that's all. You don't own me."

Johnny's eyes darkened. "No, of course not, but—"

"There's no 'but' about it." Jill firmly removed his hand from her forearm. "I'll be there tomorrow. All right?"

He stepped back so she could leave the space into which his concern had cornered her.

"It's not all right," he said, "but it'll have to do."

Worried, Johnny turned to watch her vanish among the milling people, even her hat crown swallowed in the space of a few seconds.

The Fontana brothers closed ranks on him with relief.

"Can we go back to the room now, Johnny? Nicky'll be mad that we let you make a target of yourself this way."

"I've made a target of myself, all right, but not the way you think," Johnny snapped, finally allowing himself to be herded into the elevator.

♦ ♦ ♦

By then Jill was already below the lobby, where the under-stage dressing rooms uncorked post-performance chaos by the magnum. Chorus girls screeched and chorus boys hooted. Glittering scraps of costume were tossed aside for modestly dull street garb. Casual coffee dates and assignations with all-night grocery stores were shouted across hectic community dressing rooms.

Jill raced for the Four Queens' quarters, wanting to catch Darcy before she left. She found her quarry ready to lock the dressing room door, the last one out.

"Oh, Darcy! Thank God."

"Jill. Hey, kid. What's wrong?"

"A lot. And all of it with me." Jill grabbed Darcy's slender wrist and dragged her back into the darkened room.

She flipped on the big overhead fluorescent, shut the door and pulled on Darcy's wrist until the tall woman bent down to comfortable conspiring level with Jill.

"What's wrong with you?" Darcy whispered with genuine concern.

"Everything!" Jill wailed back. Her hazel eyes greened with determination. Jill took a deep breath. "Darcy, I'm looking for a man. Or, what's worse, I've found a man. Only. . . ."

◆ ◆ ◆

The next night, two Fontana brothers stood in morose consultation in the lobby of the Crystal Phoenix, uncharacteristically immune to admiring glances from passing females.

"If we don't bring her back tonight, Johnny'll skin us alive and feed our corpses to Chef Song's carp," Aldo speculated mournfully, his mustache drooping with his eyes.

"She's gotta show tonight," Rico prophesied. "I'll drive my Camaro into that damned desert until I find her. Johnny was bad news after the show last night."

"The pits," his brother agreed. "Nicky never said this body guarding job was gonna cost us. Maybe it was that anonymous note Johnny found in the hotel safety deposit box with his diamond rings before his show. That'd kind of unnerve a guy."

Aldo snorted. "It unnerved Nicky. Hell, it even unnerved Van, and she never unnerves! They'd hoped that threatening note stuff was over." Aldo removed an ivory toothpick from the pocket of his ivory wool suitcoat and prodded contemplatively at a gold crown deep within the cavern of his mouth. "But that's not what got Johnny so steamed."

"No," his brother agreed darkly. "It was her. Who'd think a scrap of tumbleweed like her would cause us so much grief?"

"Nobody, man," Aldo sympathized. "Nobody in his right mind. But what could we do? Johnny wanted to play poker and we had to sit down with him. We're supposed to keep him happy."

"Yeah, but not at any price. When he won your brand-new six-grand Rolex . . . Jeez, Aldo, I wasn't sure whether you were gonna hand it over."

"One thing," Aldo said wisely, "Johnny sure learned to play poker in a hurry. He was a regular wild man with those cards, wasn't he? We better find her, or he'll own half this hotel before we know it."

They scanned the crowd, eyes alert for the familiar dents in a Western hat about five and a half feet off the floor. After two minutes of neck-straining surveillance, Aldo pressed his hand to Rico's forearm. "Which watch you wearing tonight, Rico?"

"Are you kidding? Some Timex I bought today at the hotel gift shop. I'm no fool." Rico checked the humble watch face dourly. "Ten minutes late. That's normal for any other dame, but not Jill O'Rourke."

"Face it, Aldo, we're on our own. She's not coming."

Aldo groaned and nervously chewed the corner of his mustache. Something plucked at the fine tailoring of his wool-blend sleeve and he spun around, annoyed.

"You can unfurl the red hankie, boys. I'm here."

Aldo looked down, as he always had to do to see Jill. He saw her. He couldn't believe it. He slapped a hand to his brother's shoulder. Rico turned, looked down, and froze.

"Holy mozzarella!"

"Holy Cinderella," Aldo echoed.

Jill slipped her arms through two of the Fontana brothers' elbows. "Duty calls," she sang out.

The trio entered the first elevator that opened. Tourists, barred from joining them by Aldo's frowning face, watched wide-eyed as Rico whisked a handkerchief over Jill's eyes just before the door closed.

"Was that what I thought it was—?" a lady from St. Louis asked her gray-haired friend.

The friend, a Las Vegas first-timer, nodded sagely. "Something kinky, dear. Definitely. It happens here all the time."

Inside the elevator, silence prevailed. Aldo and Rico escorted Jill to the usual seventh-floor door with an unusual blend of relief and anxiety.

Their knock was answered instantly. Johnny's prowling leonine presence filled the doorway, his eyes sweeping immediately to their chest level. He saw Jill at once—between them—stared and stepped inward, speechless.

Aldo put a disavowing hand on Jill's back and shoved her through the door into Johnny's suite as though pushing a laboratory mouse into a maze. Then he shut the door. Firmly.

Silence ruled the room on the other side of it.

Jill waited, hands clutching the only familiar thing on her person, the soft suede bag heavy with the weight of her revolver.

"Well?" she finally asked the silence. "Aren't you going to untie my blindfold?"

The quiet held. Then she heard the soft rasp of clothing, a shoe scraping carpet. Through the crimson blur of her blindfold, a shadow shifted from one side of her perception to the other.

"Not yet," his voice finally came, a stranger's tone in it.

Jill clasped cold hands before herself, waiting. She swallowed, hard. Darcy and she had spent six hours that afternoon walking the Las Vegas pavements smooth to find this getup. Now she was just as glad she couldn't see Jack's reaction.

"Umhmm," he hummed softly somewhere to her rear. Jill jumped. She hadn't heard him move behind her.

Something brushed the tendrils of hair at her neck. Fugitive warmth spread, inches from her skin. His presence seemed invisibly poised to envelop her.

A wild pulse fibrillated in Jill's neck. Alien breath riffled her cheek. Jack inhaled deeply at her left ear, then at her right ear a moment later.

"Uh huh." He moved around in front of her again, a blur of shape and shadow. The blot of his head lowered. Jill held tremblingly still as he bent to her throat. When he inhaled again, although she was expecting it, she gasped as if he siphoned the air he breathed from her chest.

His hands reached down for hers, then lifted them—high, higher, to his shoulders—palms up. The back of her wrists rested on velvety velour, and there was only the sound of his deep, even breathing for a long while.

Jill didn't breathe at all. Her chest felt cast in concrete, her throat mufflered in anxiety. Yet excitement fluttered at the core of her secret self.

He moved again, and she tensed. But he only bent to inhale the traces of Jungle Cat on the inside of each elbow in turn, then each wrist.

Jill waited. The uncertainty was torment, the torment exciting. She strained to read his mind, to discern his reaction from the senses left to her, from the hypersensitive surface of her skin alone.

♦ ♦ ♦

Johnny had no such handicap. Jill stood like a statue, the blindfold permitting him to study her more openly than he ever had. Johnny surveyed her with an art aficionado's lingering, loving eye, yet also with a puzzling sense of being defrauded. Everything he had come to associate with Jill had vanished, except the incongruity of her buckskin purse.

Her freshly lipsticked mouth out-crimsoned the blindfold, and her hair had been teased atop her head into a carefully disordered mop of brunet tendrils. Feather-fine wisps brushed bare shoulders, and dusky shadows defined collarbones and a well of darkness in the hollow of her throat.

The strapless red-sequined tube top she wore created a smoky cleft of cleavage. Her skirt was black velvet, fashionably short and folded protectively around the black-hosed stems of her legs like a petal. Johnny caught a rhinestone glitter inset into her hose, measured the difference in height conferred by high-piled hair and the black suede three-inch heels on which she teetered almost imperceptibly.

He took a deep breath again, part pleasure at seeing her after a night away, part discomfiture at how he felt because of how she obviously wanted him to feel.

"You look . . . lovely," he said.

The painted corners of her lips lifted, pointing to a new pink in her cheeks—not cosmetic blusher, but the admiration she had sought embarrassing her when it finally came.

She remained motionless, looking up at him despite the blindfold.

Johnny wrenched himself from his solitary consumption of the self she had presented to him and moved behind her again. His fingers worked loose the red silk-knot drawn un-intentionally tight by a startled Rico.

Jill stepped away the moment the silk slithered past her features. Johnny tossed it on the console table near the door. No jewelry adorned her except for the rhinestone wink at her ankles, and shapely ankles they were, delicate as a fawn's. They weren't the kind of ankles cowboy boots implied.

"I had a previous engagement," she lied boldly. "A party. I hope you don't mind my coming like this." She turned to face him for the first time.

Johnny read a nervous defiance in her wide-footed, tomboy stance that belied her come-hither ensemble.

"At least I'll know you have nothing up your sleeves," he noted wryly.

Jill frowned at him with eyes that had been shadowed a smoky forest green. Perhaps, the thought trapped her, she'd been naive to think that dressing like a sophisticated woman would affect a man of the world like Jack. He looked so at ease leaning against the console table, his long arms folded on his chest, his hair and eyes golden, the usual jogging suit an unusually sumptuous shade of emerald green. She suddenly suffered a case of cold feet. That's what she got for wearing shoes with less leather in them than a poodle's collar.

"Then let's play," she said brusquely. She had wanted him to look at her, and like it. Now she felt only foolish, inadequate. And her feet hurt in the $120 shoes Darcy had insisted she buy. What was she trying to prove anyway? And to whom?

She minced over to the table and braced her feet to pull

out the chair. But the narrow skirt permitted no such independent gestures. Chair legs snagged in the thick carpet, resisting until Jack's gold-dusted hand curled over the top rail and lifted it off the floor.

Jill stood facing the table while he presented the chair seat under her derrière. Her hands fidgeted angrily. She'd never needed help in sitting down before. Being a lady had its humiliations, Jill realized.

Slinging the purse to the tabletop was a familiar, reassuringly rough gesture. So was extracting the usual fresh deck of cards.

"Five-card draw?" she inquired crisply.

He nodded, sitting down, his eyes toting every nuance of her face and body language as she'd taught him. "Whatever you say."

"I'll play"—her voice went husky—"whatever you want."

He waited, frozen as a mountain lion on the brink of a desert spring. Jill felt more parched than when she had stretched full-length under the desert's glaring afternoon sun, more naked to danger than she had been under the lion's gaze.

"Five card draw," he repeated.

She slapped the deck to the table between them. He cut. She dealt. She won a hand, and won again. And again. He won. She won and won and . . . he won. She didn't care, didn't care about the march of hearts and clubs and spades and diamonds through her icy fingers.

Her voice grew curt. "Raise," she barked. "Hold pat. Deal."

Jack finally held the deck, tapping its corner on his chin. He eyed the piled ten-dollar bills on her side of the table. "Maybe we should make this more interesting."

"How?" She was incredulous.

He shrugged, fanning the cards in front of him until a golden bridge of phoenixes stretched between his spread fingers. "This is Las Vegas. We're on the Strip. Why not play strip poker?"

"No thanks. I think I played it once, very recently, and decided I didn't like it."

"Maybe you won," he suggested, his voice as thickly insinuating as honey.

"I lost," she said. Her eyes had hardened under the smoky powders shadowing them.

"Maybe you won and didn't know it."

"I know when I lose. I know when I deserve to."

"Afraid?" he inquired silkily.

"Of you?" Her dander was up. "Never!"

"Probably not," he concurred. "But tonight . . . a little."

She stretched her small tanned hand for the cards. Jack's eyes flicked to the base of her throat, where makeup couldn't quite conceal an inverted triangle of matching tan.

"If you're going to blush every time I look at you," he suggested, "maybe we'd better forget it."

"Blushes never killed anyone." Jill slapped cards down on either side of the table. "And hang onto your skivvies; I intend to take your clothes to the cleaners."

She won the first hand. Jack solemnly presented a size-thirteen kidskin loafer to the tabletop. She won the second, and he coughed up the mate.

Then he got lucky with a full house. Jill bent under the table to unhook the shoe that dangled from toes clad in sheer black silk stockings. Twenty-five dollars for a pair of pantyhose. Disgraceful! The evening sandal joined the loafers, looking like a Barbie doll accessory next to his over-size shoes.

She won next. Jack pushed back his emerald-velour

sleeve and wrenched a wide expansion bracelet of gold from his wrist.

Jill recognized the Rolex's worth and inhaled sharply. "Isn't there something less valuable you'd care to lose first?"

"You're getting me down to the nitty gritty, Miss O'Rourke, and I prefer to keep my nitty over my gritty as long as possible."

Jill fingered gold so rich it ought to have flowed over her fingers like melted butter. The inner metal still felt warm from his wrist.

"It's not fair," she said. "I'm not wearing jewelry."

"You're not going to lose, remember?"

"No, I'm not."

She won again, growing more nervous with every hand. But he kept producing jewelry like rabbits from a hat—a heavy-link gold bracelet from his other hand, a hidden chain around his neck.

The cards fell her way. She couldn't lose. She won with a pair of sevens over a pair of threes.

He sighed defeat, crossed his big golden paws to grasp the bottom of his shirt, and pulled it up over his torso and head. Jill watched the smooth unveiling of a chest aglint with a coiled aurora of hair. Patches of long silky hair glinted mysteriously under his arms as they raised to wrench the fabric over his head. Jill was reminded of being denuded of just such body hair at Delilah Darcy's meticulous attendance that afternoon. Why her and not him? Civilization made simple natural things so confusing.

Jack tossed the emerald top on the table with a grin. "This is probably big enough to serve you as a nightshirt. I imagine it gets cold nights, out on the desert."

"I've got a nightshirt," she retorted.

"Flannel, probably."

"With little red flowers all over it."

"Long," he noted sagely. "To the floor."

"Naturally."

He glanced to the cards she'd dealt while they had bantered. "Is this some new ploy? To deal cards face-up?"

Jill swept the cards back to her side of the table, glad of an excuse for the heat she could feel spreading like a brushfire over her face. The room had narrowed to the bare golden wall of the man across the table, to the claustrophobic heat and scent and sound of him.

Unnerved, she let his three tens take her pair of twos. She tossed the wraparound length of her black velvet skirt on the pile. The next hand came up four clubs. She discarded a jack of diamonds and drew a nine of hearts. Her straight had ended up crooked.

He waited politely while she wriggled out of her expensive new pantyhose under the table. They made a small shriveled pile on the table. His forefinger reached out to trace the rhinestone pattern while Jill squirmed, bottomless, against the foreign fuzzy nap of the chair seat.

"That's the way to lose," he noted, pulling the cards over to deal his turn. "From here, you look as if you haven't lost a stitch. And I look picked clean."

They flashed through his fingers, the dark cards with gilt birds on their backs, and offered Jill a paltry pair of queens. He gave himself only one card and stared at it when it came. Jill's three new cards held nothing but unrelated hearts.

"Well?" she asked, too loudly. Each had only one more article of clothing to lose.

Jack folded his cards in front of him. "I was going for a diamond straight but lost." He stood, and she watched the slowly uncoiling length of him.

His hands grabbed the waistband of the jogging pants.

Jill's eyes blinked shut, red figures dancing on the inside darkness, hearts and diamonds gone amok.

"I guess I've won," she said with a loser's quaver in her voice.

There was no answer. No sound.

Then hands clasped her arms. She screamed, softly. An alarmed shuffle began outside the door.

"Stay out," Jack bellowed.

Jill, already held against his chest, felt the powerful vibration of his words quiver against her heart. His arm, golden-downed, curved under her knees. He was carrying her somewhere, and Jill didn't dare look, but she had to wrap her arms around his neck or she would fall. Her eyes squeezed more tightly shut.

"Twin beds," Jack said ruefully. "For this I left a suite with an up-to-date king-size."

Jill finally opened her eyes to study the bedroom from the novel height of his arms, her face for once within easy reach of his.

"My bunk at home's no bigger," she said consolingly.

"But I don't have to fit in it."

Jill laughed at the mental picture of Jack in all his curried golden glory crammed into her tiny rough-walled cabin. Then she sobered. He was staring into her eyes, amusement and pleasure meeting in his face to form an expression she'd never seen before, one she wanted to capture and keep.

"You look so happy," Jill mused, running her fingers lightly over his face. It was ridiculous how, both of them almost as naked as anything that ever comes into this world, they still fixated on each other's naked faces.

"Looking isn't what makes me happy," he said pointedly.

Her palm kept his face turned to her as she leaned inward and did what she'd been afraid to do first—kiss his mouth with the tender, loving promise of her own.

Something shook Jill more than the obvious rampage of desire, something composed of push and pull, give and take, desire and delicacy. Maybe it was the careful way Jack held himself still, as if not to break a tenuous contact more touching than any firestorm of the flesh.

Jill's lips finally trembled free of his, her eyes tear-stung.

"Does kissing me always make you cry?"

"No, just now. For this moment."

"Why?" His voice was so low, she could hardly hear it. Even his breathing seemed to be frozen in a slow-motion rhythm.

"I don't know. I feel so, so . . . unlike myself. It's scary."

Impulsively, he gathered her closer. His kiss was quick, and greedy, and shaken. "But you like feeling that way?"

"I love it!"

Jack laughed and whirled her down to one of the prim twin beds. Jill muffled her shriek of surprise behind her hands.

"Yes, please refrain from bringing any more Fontana brothers down on me," Jack said. He bent to strip back the chartreuse satin coverlet, Jill reaching up to cling to his neck as he lifted her over the bedspread into the silver satin sheets beneath it.

◆ ◆ ◆

Johnny paused, one knee on the impossibly narrow bed, itself a remnant from another, less lusty age. Jill wasn't like other women, he reminded himself. She came from nowhere and lived by rules that hadn't learned to bend to the icy manipulation of cynicism.

"Jack, you've lost your poker face."

"I never had it."

"You were doing all right for a while there. Why are you afraid of me?"

"I'm afraid of hurting you."

"I'm not afraid of you." She knee-walked over the mattress to him. "Oh, I guess I thought I was." Her hands smoothed his shoulders, ran palm-down over his chest. "But I was really afraid of me. And I shouldn't be. And you shouldn't be afraid of a little thing like me."

Still he hesitated.

She only clasped him tighter. "Dammit, Jack, am I going to have to lead off on every hand? I guess I can tell you what moves to make and what cards to play in one syllable words—"

"Later." He laughed, muffling her mouth with his. "For now, let me pretend that you're a lady."

"A lady who loves you, Jack! I do, I do!"

Something warmer than desire exploded within him, a slow, spreading sensation that filled his throat and stung his eyes and echoed in his ears sweeter than the smoothest love lyric in his repertoire.

"Jill." Words seemed trite in the face of feelings so freshly coined they sizzled in the coffer of his body. Like a miser, some fear made him want to squeeze them tight between his fingers, behind his lips. Her face so near to his was rhapsodic. "I love you too."

Johnny clasped Jill tighter, feeling everything held hoarded within himself, everything that took no chances until he hardly feared even death threats, feeling that careful accumulation of himself he never shared seeping endlessly into the pitiless gravity of her loving being.

In the moment of unbidden love, Johnny's heart and mind felt the fleeting chill finger of loss and death for the first time.

◆ Midnight Louie Does a Soupcon

of Eavesdropping ◆

So what am I to do? I am simply catching a quick forty winks—all right, all right, a hundred and forty winks—on my usual chaise Louie the Thirteenth (which happens to be my, ahem, lucky number) when two of my favorite little dolls get their heads together in the Four Queens's dressing room.

It is the night of the day after the night before, a fact I am certain of, as I am taking a small dawn ramble that morning on the seventh floor when Miss Jill O'Rourke, dressed to make Fifi the Strip Tease take notice, oozes out of Room 713.

To tell the truth, I am cruising the area because Room 713 was a favorite hideaway of mine until Gentleman Johnny Diamond decided to make it his *pied-à-terre*. (This *pied-à-terre* is a masculine noun of the French sort which means a place where a fellow hangs out; I am full of the old *française* since joining the staff of a high-class joint like the Crystal Phoenix.)

Anyway, Gentleman Johnny has muscled in on my territory, so to speak. I always feel a great rapport with the past when catnapping in Suite 713; besides, its color scheme matches my eyes. So I hang around and hope, which is how I happen to catch Miss Jill O'Rourke ankling—and I do mean ankling of the first water—out of 713 so late in the evening it is early in the morning, if you catch my drift.

The Fontana boys are snoozing on two folding chairs in

the hall, it is so late. Were I the Poison Pen Fan—and I am not, as my penmanship is not what it used to be—I could be in and out of the room with enough missives to over-whelm a bureaucrat and nobody any the wiser. So the boys jump to attention and re-bandana Miss Jill O'Rourke's bright little eyes, which this morning are as dreamy as a shot of Scotch Mist.

It takes no genius to figure out what has been going on, and the Fontana boys cannot refrain from making with the knowing smirks. Miss Jill O'Rourke notices this rather noxious tendency in human behavior and tightens her little hands on her buckskin purse before the boys can slip the handkerchief over her eyes and says like this:

"I know what you two are thinking and if you continue in this vein for more than two more seconds it will be the last thought you will ever contemplate, as I will perform a small censorial operation on your cerebral cortexes with my forty-five revolver."

Perhaps she phrases it a bit less delicately but the im-port is the same.

I am relieved to see Miss Jill O'Rourke is assuming her regular aplomb despite dalliances of a romantic nature and despite being dressed like the cutest little French cream puff to hit a boutique bakery.

So I play informal escort as the boys guide her back to the lobby, where she does a vanishing act. I retire to my second favorite retreat—the dressing room inhabited for seven hours a night six nights a week by the Four Queens.

Here I withdraw further to my own dreams of a sen-suous nature, fondly recalling lady loves I have courted, ri-vals I have scratched off the map, and my widespread, numerous, and thankfully unknown offspring.

Before I know it, it is late afternoon and the dressing

room is buzzing. It seems I have awakened in the middle of a debate between Miss Jill O'Rourke and Miss Darcy McGill Austen.

"I will not take it back; it is yours," says Miss Darcy McGill Austen.

"I have thought it over. It is not 'me.' Give it to some broke chorus girl."

"None of them are little enough to fit into your gear," Miss Darcy McGill retorts. "Jill, we spent hours looking for this stuff. What is the matter, did it not work?"

"Oh, it worked," Miss Jill O'Rourke says bitterly. "But what do I do for an encore?"

She takes the Piggly Wiggly grocery bag she is carrying and slams it to the dressing table top. There is not much "slam" in it, as it is packed full of delicacies of a female nature. The bag falls over, spilling a red sequined circle of elastic onto one of my ears.

Even I can apprehend that I look silly in the mirror.

"Oh, Louie!" Miss Darcy McGill Austen laughs, thereby lowering some of the high regard in which I hold her. "You look silly."

At least she removes this embarrassing article of apparel. She turns to Jill and shakes her by her buckskinned shoulders until every fringe on her back is in danger of suffering a whiplash.

"Jill, you can be any way you want to be, plain jeans or fancy duds, they're different sides of you and I think they both have their heart set on the same thing. It is not what anyone else thinks of you, it is what you think of yourself."

Miss Jill O'Rourke squares her shoulders and folds her arms in the feisty way for which she is noted and loved.

"I think I owe somebody an apology," she says, and marches out of the room.

I must confess that I am not visited with overhearing so juicy a conversation since the maid left on the penthouse television while I was stealing a discreet snooze under Mr. Nicky Fontana's bed and my ears were blessed with a short exchange from the daytime television drama, "Lays of Our Lives." Perhaps I misheard the title. My ears are not what they used to be, and then again, I have been told I have a back-alley mentality.

♦ Chapter Seven ♦

No one occupied the elevator Jill took to the seventh floor. Even the hallway was empty, not surprising for seven o'clock of a Las Vegas evening. Everyone alive in Las Vegas would be eating, drinking, and making merry with dice, cards, and coins on ground-floor levels all along the Strip.

Jill shut her eyes and turned resolutely right, as she'd always turned when escorted to Johnny's room. She began pacing out the carefully counted steps she had mentally measured since the first time the Fontana boys had brought her here blindfolded.

". . . eighty-five, six, seven." She paused, took a deep breath, and opened her eyes.

A door confronted her, a door like any other along the hallway. On its plain face hung a brass number. "Seven-one-three," Jill intoned to herself.

She shrugged and knocked. No answer came. She pushed on the door, then jiggled the knob anyway, knowing it was locked. Maybe it was the wrong room, she thought. Maybe it was the right one, but he wasn't in there. No one was in there. Did he come only to this room in the early morning hours, and only to meet her?

The notion chilled her bones. Phantom lover. The corny phrase crept upon her unawares from the hall's endless shadows.

"Jack!" The flat of her hand hit the door in perplexed frustration.

It pushed ajar.

Jill stepped back, pulling her purse in front of her hip

and slipping her hand to the revolver butt inside.

"Open sesame," she teased the door. Nothing happened, and she breathed easier. There was no mystery to why it had sprung open. The lock must be the original one, old and unreliable. Like us, her grandfather would say if he'd heard her think such a thing. Like me and the boys.

"Nonsense," Jill told herself, in response to what, she didn't know.

She edged into the room and, sighing into the silence that hung as heavy as the satin drapes, shut the door behind her. The light switch on the right clicked at her touch, forcing warm light through the silken silver shade of a floor-lamp across the room.

It was the same place, neatly tidied, where she had always seen him. The game-table top shone in the soft lamp-light, cleared now of abandoned clothes and cards. A desk across the room invited her, but when she slid open its drawers, time-faded papers and out-of-date fountain pens slid together in abandoned disarray.

She picked up crumbly-edged documents naming one "Hezekiah Joseph Jackson." Jack? she wondered wildly. But the signature's handwriting trailed off in the same ancient, spidery slant as Encyclopedia's. Hezekiah Joseph Jackson must be long gone.

Then who was Jack, and why did he meet her here, where he obviously didn't live? And what right had she to ask those questions of anyone? She who always kept her own cards so close to the vest, they served as impervious pasteboard armor?

Jill moved into the bedroom, freezing to find both beds made. What phantom maid had invaded hers and Jack's territory? Is that what fewer than twenty-four hours can make of what had seemed a timeless, selfless interlude, a remade bed?

131

Jill had never wondered such things, had never stopped to think about anything more than her frequent pilgrimages between Glory Hole and the Strip, between isolation and crowded isolation.

She sat on the chartreuse coverlet, her palm caressing the satin sheen and her fingers tracing the quilting stitches. Then she leaned over to see if the dust ruffle allowed a pair of size thirteen shoes to peek from beneath the bed. No, no trace of Jack shared the room with Jill but her memories.

"It's strange," Jill said aloud, to the room, to herself. "Strange that I don't know who he is or what he really wants. Strange that it doesn't . . . matter."

Talking aloud in the room was less crazy than it sounded. Something seemed to heed Jill; the walls were waiting. The curtains hung solemnly, their silver folds like long grey beards falling from wise, invisible heads.

We have heard it all, the slick folds seem to rustle upon each other with the subtle hum of the air-conditioning vent. We have seen it all. Don't worry.

Jill got up and opened the closet door with its cold, old-fashioned glass knob. Empty padded hangers, variously covered by rose, forest-green, and chartreuse satin, swayed together in the artificial draft she'd created.

Where were the jogging suits, a different color for every evening? The comb, the toothbrush, the electric razor? Where was Jack?

A clock on the night stand between the twin beds read almost eight, in strange, old-fashioned numbers. Jill could go downstairs and play at the public tables until midnight or later, but her mind wouldn't be on the cards. She'd have to wait—here.

Jill studied the matching beds, then tossed her hat atop the pillows of the other one, the one as yet undisturbed by any haunting memories, and lay on her side across the pristine satin coverlet. She pulled a deck of cards from her jacket pocket, shuffled expertly, and began laying out a nine-row solitaire pattern, the hardest of any to win.

Jill forgot the ghosts that haunted her and this room. The cards took up most of the narrow bed that she herself wasn't occupying. She began the first game by moving the yellow-haired Jack of diamonds onto a poker-faced queen of spades and looking next for the ten of hearts.

◆ ◆ ◆

"Then where the hell is she?"

Johnny's demand began loudly in the public arena of the hall and hushed as he charged into the privacy of the room. "It's way past one."

Aldo and Ralph Fontana shadowed him haplessly.

"She didn't show tonight, Johnny. Honest! We waited at the regular spot. We waited the whole time you were held up after the show by that press interview. We can't bring you something that isn't there!"

"She's got to be there."

"She didn't come the night before last," Aldo put in logically. "Maybe she's on an every-other-night schedule."

"She would have said something."

"Not necessarily," Ralph said. "Jill O'Rourke isn't used to explaining herself to anybody."

"She would have to me!" Johnny's eyes blazed, as hot as a shooting star.

Comparatively cooler Italian temperaments backed off in unison.

"Say, Johnny, we'll go down again, look some more. Hey, we don't wanna miss her, man."

"I'm here."

Jill stood in the bedroom doorway, hat and boots off, jacket gone, wearing only jeans and a pearl-snapped checked shirt. She looked small and sleepy and something else.

"Jill." Johnny's voice dropped dramatically in tone and pitch in the course of that one word. Such vocal tricks made him the consummate on stage balladeer he was, but this time genuine emotion achieved the special effect.

Nowhere in the room's expectant silence was there a niche for a pair of misplaced Fontana brothers. They slunk to the door in tandem, feeling both relieved and outraged.

"How'd she find out the room number?" Aldo, the elder, grumbled aloud. "That blows security."

"Maybe your pocket hankie sprung a leak," Ralph suggested.

"Maybe Johnny spilled it."

Johnny was staring at Jill, ignoring the charge.

She stared back at him, but she heard every word they uttered. "I found it myself. It'd take a lot more than a blindfold to keep me from knowing where I am."

"You can go," Johnny said over his shoulder.

They went and set up shop outside the door.

Johnny kept staring at Jill, looking happy, worried, and surprised at the same time. "Jill, why on earth did you come up here on your own? Simply to show them you could?"

"No. I just couldn't wait to see you, *Johnny*."

The words were so welcome, he hardly perceived the stinger in the scorpion's tail.

"I should hope not," he began playfully, moving toward her, all his worry warmed over into relieved affection. Then he stopped. "What did you call me?"

Her dark head jerked toward the exit. "What they did. Or aren't I allowed to?"

"No, it's not that. It's—stupid, really."

"Is that your name? Johnny?"

"Sometimes."

"Oh, can it! I was fit to be tied, coming up to say *I* was a fraud, and here you are, going around under separate identities."

" 'Jack' and 'Johnny' are hardly separate identities. And exactly what fraud did you commit last night? Are you married?"

"No!" She glared at him indignantly, then saw by the rays of amusement around his eyes that the question had been deliberately provoking.

Jill turned sideways to lean back against the bedroom doorframe so she didn't have to see him face-to-face. She addressed the chrome hinge high on the doorframe opposite.

"I'm a fraud because fancy clothes and needle heels and mousse on my hair and cologne on my elbows isn't me. I just did it because . . . because you weren't doing anything . . . more . . . after you started in on kissing me. And I figured, maybe if I looked more like those female shills the management puts down by the gaming tables to lure the high rollers, you might get the idea.

"I've seen 'em, those women. I know they dress that way because it . . . works. I guess it does, and I'm not sorry it did, but I can't do it again. I just don't know how to play that game." She looked painfully at him. "And I hate to lose. I hate to lose like anything."

He stationed himself against the opposite doorframe. The doorway wasn't that wide; two made a crowd. Jill carefully focused just past his right ear.

"Jill . . . ah, it is Jill, isn't it?"

"Why, you lying—*two-name!* You're the one who's put on

the act! You know my name and you've seen my territory from Searchlight to Jackpot!"

"I presume those are communities at one end of Nevada and another?" He was chuckling.

"Damn right they are! And those are the names they've gone by since they got started. They didn't switch around and call themselves Flashlight and Kingpot at the drop of a jogging suit."

He threw his head back and laughed. Jill, despite her best intentions, found herself mesmerized by a mouthful of molars with no visible fillings. Maybe the phony teeth should have tipped her off, she admonished herself.

"Jill, for Pete's sake—or Jack's sake! They call me Johnny. It's a pretty silly name for a man in his thirties, but I'm stuck with everybody knowing me by that name. Is it so wrong to want to be Jack with someone new?"

"Not if that's all it is. I'd call you Wilfred if you wanted me to and if I was sure you weren't hiding something from me, something—Where do you really live? And what do you do? And who's . . . after you? The Fontana boys don't pick their teeth outside your door night after night for nothing."

"Nothing important, Jill. Less than you hide from the world."

"What do you mean?"

"Don't get mad at me again; you were just melting nicely. I swear I got a whiff of some perfume you don't like to wear." Her expression darkened further, this time in angry admission. "But I asked about you. 'Where does she live? Why doesn't she want anyone to know where she lives, or with whom? Why is she so mum, aside from sketchy mentions of her grandfather and his old war buddies? Why didn't she go to school? Why will she tell me more about an old boyfriend than where she goes home at night?' "

"None of your business!"

"There. You see, you answered your own questions."

"Then I guess we haven't got much to say to each other." Jill angrily pushed away from the doorjamb.

Johnny's long arm barred her way, thrust across her path.

Jill stopped abruptly on the brink of crashing into it. Her narrowed eyes, Colt-.45 cold, traveled up the length of his arm to his shoulder and face. He looked very sure of himself.

"We don't have much to say to each other," he conceded. "Not at a time like this."

"A time like what?"

"When you're about to say how much you missed me."

"I wasn't. I wouldn't miss you if you were the ace of hearts and I held a king-high flush."

"And I was about to say how much I'd missed you, and that I'd been thinking about you all day, all night, and was just waiting to see you again, wearing whatever you damn please and hopefully damn little of it."

"Oh!" She shook her head in speechless fury, her teeth gritted behind taut lips and revolver smoke coiling in her eyes.

He smiled the slow sheepish smile of a lion about to indulge in a romp and spread his arms wide, releasing her.

Jill poised like a cat to flee, then suddenly turned on him and launched herself at his neck. Johnny felt no fear for his well-being but caught and lifted her in his arms so she could wrap her legs around his waist as tightly as her arms clung to his neck.

"Oh, you big fraud!" Jill exclaimed in exuberant reunion. "I missed you, too, whatever your name is."

"It's whatever you call me at the moment, that's what it is. The rest is all . . . phantoms."

Jill lifted her head from his shoulder. "It's strange you should say that."

"Why?"

"That's what I was feeling in this suite while I was waiting for you, all around me—phantoms."

"I'm not one." He squeezed her so hard, she thought her ribs would collapse. "And you're the firmest phantom I've ever encountered." He turned them to face the bedroom. "Dealer's choice. Bed number one, or bed number two?"

Jill sighed. "J-Johnny."

"Is that what you've decided on?" She nodded solemnly. "Why?"

"I don't want you to keep me apart from the life you lead any more than you have. I've lived apart all my life. I don't want to be any farther from you than the laws of physics will allow."

"You've got it," he promised, bringing her once more to a narrow bed in an old-fashioned room filled with phantoms, or the traces of one.

They made desperate love, frightened by how close they had come to cheating themselves of this closeness, then slow, certain love. Clothes were the least of their concerns and melted away, unnoticed. Names faded to throaty murmurs, then feline purrs and satisfied growls.

"Oh! I hear—" Jill blinked her eyes at the dimly seen ceiling, clasping Johnny closer than her own skin, "I hear slot machines!"

"Romantic hellion, aren't you? You've got gambling on the brain."

"No, listen!"

A slow, sliding chink rang musically beneath them.

Johnny leaned over the bed's side and jerked up the silver-satin dust ruffle. A random chime sounded again.

Then another. Then a cascade of them, chattering together faster and faster.

Johnny rolled off the bed and went down on his knees beside it. "Turn up the lamp, will you?"

With two quick clicks, light flooded the nightstand. Jill slipped to the floor beside him, then wriggled under the dust ruffle until only her bottom protruded.

"Johnny, what's cold . . . and round, and comes in bunches?"

"Frozen grapes?" he wondered, studying the carving on the nightstand.

"Money! Gold! Coins . . . look!"

She backed out from under the bed, her arms sweeping booty into the light. Coins big as plums tumbled out.

Johnny plucked one and held it up to the lamp.

"Not gold—silver. Silver dollars. Jill"—he pushed himself up against the opposite bed—"these are old coins. Old, uncirculated . . . my gosh, Carson City silver dollars! These must be worth a mint! They're worth The Mint downtown. They're . . . they shouldn't be here."

She fell back on the bed, her hands dribbling the coins onto the coverlet, laughing. "It's a treasure! Our treasure. Just think: if we hadn't switched beds, nobody'd ever have found them. What a jackpot! How crazy. Johnny, you know I think somebody up there likes us!"

He tapped one of the coins against his phony teeth, checking for genuineness. "There must be a story behind this cache. I'll talk to Nicky and Van in the morning. Meanwhile, maybe we should get some sleep."

"Not yet." Jill twisted onto the floor and wedged herself under the bed again. Her voice came, muffled but determined, from beyond the dust ruffle. "There's no way I'm gonna leave an uncollected pot uncounted under the table. I won't sleep a wink until I tote up our take."

"All of it?" he asked, nonplussed.

"Every last dollar," she said, shoveling out pile after pile of gleaming silver.

"I like money as much as the next guy, but this is not my idea of how to spend an exciting evening."

Jill popped out, undeterred. "Sleep then, you big galoot. I'll be in the counting house!"

She bent to pull on her jeans and shirt, then stood and snatched a silver satin pillowcase from the other bed. Big silver dollars rattled into their high-fashion moneybag as fast as small, tanned hands could funnel them.

Johnny was reaching for his own clothes. "I have a feeling love has just lost out to money."

"No, it hasn't. It's just that money takes counting and love doesn't. Want to help?"

His smiling face vanished into the folds of his velour shirt as he pulled it down over his head. By the time he followed her to the outer room, Jill had the coins spilled out on the floral carpet and was sitting amidst them like a child surrounded by pieces of a Tinkertoy paradise on Christmas morning.

◆ Chapter Eight ◆

Silver dollars, shiny as the finish on Nicky Fontana's new platinum-colored Corvette, rose in towering piles of twenty, forming a high-rise skyline across the card table.

"How many are there?" Nicky wondered.

Johnny rubbed a hand over his eyes and consulted a sheet of Crystal Phoenix notepaper. "An even thousand, minus one. I gave, uh, someone a good luck piece. I suppose I can get it back if I have to, if I'm legally required to turn in every last piece of loot."

"Legally, we'd better consult an attorney and keep quiet about this," Van said.

Nicky turned to stare. "Van von Rhine suggesting we be less than forthright about our find? Think what kind of publicity the hotel will get!"

"I *am* thinking about the publicity." She walked to the windows, her muted blond head contrasting with the silver drapes serving as her backdrop. "I'm thinking about Johnny's safety, too. We still have this madman on the loose. These coins must be very old. We should find out where they might be from before we do anything rash, like calling the police."

"Makes sense." Nicky grinned. "Maybe they're something Jersey Joe Jackson tucked away for a rainy day. I bet he didn't have any heirs, not if the hotel had to bury him." He glanced to Johnny. "You say they were hidden in the mattress?"

"The springs." Johnny led them to the bedroom threshold, where they all stood staring into the room, reluc-

141

tant to confront the puzzle too closely.

"Which bed?" Van asked.

"The right."

"Did you—check—the left bed?" Nicky didn't quite know how to phrase it.

Everyone was studiously avoiding the details of how the money had happened to shower them with its sudden presence.

"That one's normal; we tried it last ni—" Johnny retreated from trampling directly on the truth. "I spent a half hour under the other bed before I called you this morning. It's got nothing to hide but rusty springs."

The trio contemplated the scene of the crime in silence.

"And you only gave one coin to Jill?" Van asked absently.

A longer silence prevailed. During it, Van's blue eyes suddenly widened in self-reproach.

"Right," Johnny finally admitted.

Silence.

"Say, she's a great girl," Nicky put in nervously.

"Woman," Johnny corrected.

"Right," Nicky said. "You'll have to bring her upstairs to dinner with us sometime. But no cards afterwards, not even a friendly game. That little . . . woman'll take you down to your last, er, silver dollar."

"Actually," Johnny said, "I've beaten her at poker."

"You have?" Nicky was awestruck.

"Don't worry, Nicky. I just have a secret weapon: I affect her concentration."

"Nice work if you can get it."

"You two!" Van linked arms with them and drew them back into the living room. "Why can't men just say, 'Hey, are you interested in Jill?' 'Hell, yes.' Women are much more open with each other. Look, Johnny," she went on.

"We're glad if you've found somebody to make your off-stage hours sing. It's really none of our business. But those silver dollars are. Officially, they're hotel property."

"Easy come, easy go," quipped Johnny.

"Don't laugh, brother," Nicky put in seriously. "You may be rolling in green pasta, but those dollars could be worth enough to make even you gulp. They could go for ten, twenty times their face value."

Johnny's mouth tightened. "I don't give a fig for 'hotel property.' Jill found them. And I've got a feeling she could use them."

"First we'll have a numismatist check one," Van promised. "If no one has a claim on them, they're yours. The Crystal Phoenix rakes in enough 'treasure' at the craps tables; we don't need every mattress hoard."

Nicky rolled his dark eyes to the ceiling. "Listen to the woman. She gives away money like it was Jawbreakers and threatens to consult some kinky fortune teller with a four-syllable name."

"A numismatist is an expert on coins," Van said. "And it's easy to give away what you never had. We'll send someone—"

"My brothers," Nicky specified firmly.

"—to pick up the coins and store them in the hotel vault until we can solve this puzzle."

On the way out, Van paused by the desk. "Maybe there's some clue, an invoice or something, among these old papers."

"Sure." Johnny saw them to the door, waved goodbye, nodded to the current duo of Fontanas on guard duty and retreated back into the suite.

He yawned, stretched and then, feeling both lazy and useless, moved to the desk and began pulling pieces of paper from the drawers into which they were jammed.

♦ ♦ ♦

"Where did you get this?"

Eightball shook the silver dollar in Jill's face, as if confronting her with evidence of a childish misdeed.

She hesitated in answering, which wasn't characteristic of the forthright Jill. Her grandfather's arthritis-curled fingers clawed into her shoulder. That wasn't characteristic either.

"Damn it, Jilly! It's important. Tell me!"

"Ned," Pitchblende rebuked in his deep, sorrowful voice.

Nobody ever called Eightball by his given name.

The silver dollar spun to the rough tabletop as Eightball tossed it there, and turned like a top. Every eye fixed upon it—Wild Blue's, Pitchblende's, Encyclopedia's, Spuds's, even Eightball's. Jill watched it, too, trying to buy time.

"I . . . won it off a fellow," she began, her throat half smothering the lie. She'd meant only to brandish the coin as a curiosity, not to confess her sins. But to tell the truth . . . about Jack/Johnny, about the funny old twin beds and what they'd been doing on them—it wouldn't work, she thought.

Eightball and the boys consoled themselves for the strange life they'd brought her up to lead by thinking of her as a child. Now was not the time to hand them proof to the contrary.

"Where'd he get it?" Eightball wanted to know next.

"He didn't say! It's just money. Funny old money. I thought you guys'd get a kick out of seeing it. I heard they used to play in Vegas with silver dollars, but I'd never seen one. I thought it'd make a good lucky piece."

"It's not just money, Jilly," Encyclopedia was explaining patiently, as if she were the child they thought her, that they insisted on keeping her. "This is a rare coin, worth way more than its face value." His age-set eyes took spry measure of his pals. "Where there's one, there's got to be others."

"Oh." Is that all they wanted, Jill thought, to know that this was only one of a whole slew of coins? "Now that you mention it, the man said he'd found a whole bunch of these somewhere."

"Where?" Pitchblende was no longer her advocate but her interrogator.

"In . . . in a bed."

"A bed?" Eightball's voice rang incredulously. He reminded Jill of a fire-and-brimstone minister working himself up to full power in a Sunday sermon.

"In a hotel, the Crystal Phoenix. He said they just fell out of the mattress. Onto the floor. Piles of them."

"What man? Did you get his name?" Encyclopedia asked eagerly.

Sort of, Jill thought wryly. Part of it. In two versions. What was Johnny's last name? How could she have made love to a man whose name she didn't know? How could she defend that to anyone, much less these five old men so alien from her and now so unexpectedly fierce?

"No, no name," she answered. Their untidy eyebrows lowered sourly, en masse. Pity made her want to strew a few breadcrumbs in their paths. "But he was staying in a funny room. All old-fashioned, he said, with chartreuse counterpanes and wallpaper, like from the Forties. You know, even the curtain valances were swept up in coiling shapes, like Betty Grable wears her hair on your 1943 calendar, Wild Blue."

"Forties-style." Eightball reached for the silver dollar and cradled it in his line-laced palm. He glanced at the others from under a hedge of iron-gray eyebrows. "Fits the time factor. D'you suppose Hez got funny with some of the money?"

"Nah." Pitchblende sounded certain. "He was biding his time, just like the rest of us. He happened to get lucky on Las Vegas real estate after the war is all. Then he forgot about us. And the money. Didn't need either of us."

"*He* buried it." Spuds's voice came sour and even more certain. "He might have nipped some out. How d'you suppose he bought those first acres, even if desert land was sand-cheap then? And he lived in that hotel suite all those years, at the Joshua Tree."

"If only we had the map," Wild Blue put in. "See these bloodshot lines in my eyeballs? I've flown over that terrain until every dip of it's engraved on my eye whites. If I could find the lost camel, why—we'd be in like Flynn."

"He's dead," Encyclopedia said suddenly, his eyes tight behind his trifocals. "And most of us will be, soon enough. Maybe it's fitting that fate throws one of these dollars into Jilly's jackpot some night. Maybe that's all we'll ever see of it."

Jill stared from familiar face to familiar face. They seemed to be speaking Martian.

"What are you guys talking about? It doesn't make any sense. You talk like it was your money."

Eightball's fist clenched on the silver dollar. "It ain't. We might wish it was, but it ain't."

He laughed, opened his fingers, and let the coin fall from his hand to the tabletop. "You take it, Jill; it's your winnings. Pay no attention to our gabbing. We're just a bunch of lost old men chasing dusty old dreams that weren't ever ours by right in the first place."

"Don't say that!" she objected. "If . . . if a person can't

chase dreams, then what's the use?"

Jill stood up, feeling as ready to run from them as she had when she'd first beaten Eightball at poker. The childish tears that must not escape at any cost stung her eyes. In a moment her nose would redden and all her brave independence would sink into a sea of self-pity.

They all stared at her sadly, no answers in their faded eyes. She saw them as Johnny would see them, or Darcy. Weird old guys who'd dropped out from real life long ago, who'd hitched their wagons to one stubborn star and hung on until no one but they saw it.

"You were out again all night," her grandfather said gruffly. "What's wrong, Jilly? We don't need that much money to get by that you have to play all night. Maybe you should stay out of Vegas awhile."

"Yeah." Spuds came forward with an eager grin. "You could help me with the grub. A girl should learn to cook."

"No! It's too late! I play cards. That's what I do." She grabbed her hat and spread her hand over the silver dollar. No one challenged her for it. "That's what I'll keep on doing."

Her fist clamped shut on the oversized coin, on as much of it as her small fingers could hold, and she left for her cabin, walking when she wanted to run, feeling rebellious and knowing she was scared.

In her own room, she searched for a place to store her unlucky lucky piece. Finally she laid it on her treasure board and set the bottle of perfume on it, as if it were a pedestal. There was no mirror in the room; Jill had never missed one before. She knew she probably looked tired and pale and more than a little puzzled.

She threw herself on the bed, scratching her palm back and forth on the rough wool, denim, and cotton patchwork quilt. It rubbed her the wrong way for the first time; there was no wrong way to rub on satin, she thought.

Why did her grandfather and the others get so excited over one old silver dollar? Why did they start thinking of keeping her away from town, from Johnny—although they couldn't know about him?

Maybe, Jill thought, her heart sinking into the scuffed toes of her cowboy boots, maybe . . . Johnny knew more about the coins than he let on. *Think about it,* she told herself, sitting on the cot. *A man without a last name, with the run of a fancy hotel like the Crystal Phoenix, with bodyguards outside the door. Maybe Johnny was mob. Maybe someone was out to hit him. Maybe she was just a wild card that had got thrown into a hand somebody had dealt long ago.*

Jill wrung her hands, racked by uncertainty. None of them were what they seemed, Johnny or the boys. One thing was certain: She couldn't relieve her confusion by confiding to either camp about the other. As far as the boys knew, Johnny did not exist. As far as she dare tell Johnny, her grandfather and his friends were distant, dotty old coots, vague blotches of local color.

A lone tear pooled at the corner of her eye and indulged itself in a painstakingly slow ramble down her cheek. Jill let its track mark her face for a minute, as if a tear was to be her only treasure, before she dashed it away with the back of her hand.

◆ ◆ ◆

"Here." Jill threw the silver dollar down on the game table between herself and Johnny. She had come to the room that night, going through all the motions of their card-playing ritual. Johnny had decided to humor her pride or her perversity, whichever drove her.

"You can keep it," he said. "For luck."

"I don't need luck. I'm a professional, remember?"

"For love, then."

She tilted back her hat brim so her eyes weren't in shadow. "Are you free to give love, Johnny?"

"I thought so. Are you free to take it?"

"I don't know."

"Jill, what's wrong? Look, I know we met in a bizarre way. In some ways, I lead a bizarre life. But so do you. It couldn't have been any other way. And for now, I'm stuck in this damn endless rut like a phonograph needle in a groove. I just go round and round. Work late, play later. . . ."

"What *is* your job, Johnny?" Jill asked, her eyes lowered as she dealt the first hand.

"I—" He thought a bit, then smiled ironically. "I guess I make people happy. I sell moods. Permit them to go someplace special, see and hear something unique in their experience."

"But what exactly do you *do*? How do you make all the money that buys the loyalty that stands guard outside your door, that pays for Rolex watches? By the way, look under your pillow. I put it back, as a lucky piece. What's your occupation, Johnny?"

"Occupation." He laughed. "It's hardly that. I don't want to think about it, Jill, not when I'm with you. I want you to take me away from it, my workaday nighttime world. We've got something magical, don't you see? Our relationship is outside the everyday patterns of our separate lives. We're lost in some Never-Never Land. Here, in this suite, we're simply . . . us."

"So." Jill picked up her five cards and fanned them into a tight hand. "You deal drugs."

"Hell no!" He stared at her expressionless face. "You

can't begin to believe that."

"Why not? You don't want to tell me what you do. You must be ashamed of it. But you make money at it. Enough so somebody wants to—" her flat tones faltered, "is trying to hurt you. I've been around Vegas long enough to know what goes down all over this town. Why should you be any different? How many cards?" she finished in businesslike tones.

Johnny's hands swept across the table to encompass hers.

"You'll wrinkle the cards," Jill pointed out tonelessly.

"I'll tear the cards to smithereens and toss 'em off the fourteenth floor!" His eyes smoldered like a hungry coyote's.

"I'm armed," she warned.

"Not without your hands free," he answered, his eyes narrowing.

They sat glaring at one another, Jill resentfully aware of how completely Johnny's hands encompassed hers, of how truly their intense, warm intervention disarmed her.

Johnny watched her through a thick translucent pane of cooling emotions, his superior force balked, even before it began to assert itself, by how contrary Jill could be when she felt she had to. Every additional second of their Mexican standoff reminded him that mere custody fell far short of the way he wanted to hold Jill to him, to his life and his future. But he wouldn't, couldn't, let go.

"Is what you do, sell dreams, not dreamdust, honest?" she finally asked.

"Absolutely," he swore.

"Then why have you got me in a fistlock?"

His fingers loosened slightly. "My hands are cold. But not as cold as your nerve."

"Whoever lets go first loses," she proposed, an impish smile suddenly brightening her impassive face.

Johnny smiled back and leaned forward until his forearms rested on the table. "Then we could be here all night."

"What's new?"

"So let's talk. Why are you suddenly so worried about my so-called occupation?"

"Because I'm tired of people who won't tell me anything about themselves! I don't like mysteries. I make my living finding out what's in the cards, not concealing it."

"You know I love you," he suggested gently.

Jill stared at his face, her visual inventory immediately turning personal. Before she had known Johnny, nothing about him would have ranked on her favorite-features list. Now, it all came together in a harmony created to touch her to the quick, endearing and exciting in equal doses.

His hands were large and warm, and she didn't really mind their taking command of hers, not even when the deck had given her four of a kind right off and now they'd have to reshuffle the cards and deal all over again.

"I'm afraid, Johnny," she admitted. "I don't know how to help you."

"Be there. Be here," he said.

"Every night? I can't go on like this, playing hooky. I've got a living to earn."

"You yourself said I've got money to burn."

"I'll win it, but I won't take it. And playing poker with you is like stealing sand from the Mojave. I figure we better give it up, permanently."

"There are better things to do," he conceded.

"And that's another thing." She frowned and pulled back her hands. Johnny's opened like a big golden sunflower to let hers go.

"Where is that . . . going? I love you, but I don't know you."

"It's better than the other way around."

"Maybe." Jill leaned back in the chair and squinted suspiciously at him. "Why are you so calm about this? Why aren't you raging and growling like some cranky old mountain lion?"

Johnny's yellow eyes blinked; then he growled, a deep bass growl that ran up and down the scale in theatrically impressive arpeggios, and pounced.

"Johnny! Let me go! Let me down!" Jill screeched obligingly, viewing the world unbalanced over his shoulder.

"Lions never let go of prey," he said. "Particularly if they've just been called old and cranky right to their grizzled muzzles."

Jill lurched precariously, and the room with her, as he turned. "Where are you going?"

"To my cave."

The bedroom door tilted drunkenly into her sights, the lintel perilously close to her hat crown.

"Johnny, I won't make it through. My hat—"

Across the room, the doorknob rattled urgently. "Johnny, hey, Johnny! You all right in there?"

He sobered instantly. "Fine," he yelled. "Just celebrating a winning hand. Hold your firepower."

"We're supposed to say that Van and Nicky are coming to see you," a Fontana shouted back.

"Now?"

"In a minute or so. The bellman just left with the message."

Johnny bent to let Jill slide off his shoulder to her feet.

"Van and Nicky!" Jill looked around frantically. "We'd better get back to playing cards!"

Johnny caught her hand and dragged her to the door, which he unlocked.

"Forget it, sweet. Van and Nicky know all about us."

"You told them?"

"They figured it out." He pulled her down on the sofa beside him. "Take off your hat and make yourself comfortable." Johnny's hand sent the hat flying across the room, where it landed on a lampshade.

"I feel naked without my hat," she protested, patting her bare head with anxious hands.

"A nice way to feel," Johnny returned, pulling her close. Someone knocked.

"I'll get rid of them fast," Johnny whispered in her ear.

On his invitation, the door opened. Nicky Fontana and Van von Rhine walked in to find Johnny and Jill sitting side by literal side on the couch. Neither seemed surprised.

"Hello, Jill," Van said calmly, inclining her regal satin-blond bead. Nicky grinned his silent greetings before turning to Johnny.

Jill swallowed. To her, Nicky Fontana and Van von Rhine, owners of the Crystal Phoenix, were elevated beings, like angels. They shouldn't, couldn't be nodding at her like equals.

Van sat alone on the long floral sofa. Nicky pulled out the desk chair for himself.

"We hate to bother you, Johnny, but we figured you'd be up still," Nicky began, then stopped, then rushed on. "Anyway, Van got an evaluation on that jackpot you found. Tell him."

"Jill found it," Johnny insisted. "She could hear a slot machine pay off at forty paces."

"Tell them, then," Nicky repeated patiently.

Van sat forward to begin what was obviously to be a full-blown story.

"They're genuine, all right—1879 silver dollars, never

153

circulated, coined at Carson City before the mint there was closed. And they're worth what Nicky said they were, up to ten thousand times their face value."

"You're rich!" Johnny told Jill, squeezing her shoulders.

"But"—everyone looked at Van as she dropped the fatal discouraging word into the recipe—"I'm afraid they've got a tangled history. They were involved in a train robbery back in the forties. The early casinos liked to encourage players to use silver dollars. One of them was shipping these in for a display gimmick. But the train was robbed. Thousands of silver dollars were taken. They've never showed up since."

"In fact"—she looked reluctantly at Jill—"I'll have to ask for the one you have back. It's, ah, evidence."

Jill got up quickly, too quickly, but Johnny didn't notice.

"It's here," she said from the game table, turning with a glint of silver in her hand. "I'd brought it back already."

"Great!" Nicky met her half way to take the coin. "Maybe there's a reward."

Johnny was leaning forward on the sofa, rapt at Van. "A train robbery! That sounds like the Old West. And they never caught who took them?"

"Nope," Nicky said. "Although they're beginning to think Jersey Joe Jackson, late of this very suite, may have known something about it. He was a shady character before the war; nothing major, but after it, he was rich."

"Wow. I love it!" Johnny sat back on the chartreuse couch, his arms spread wide along its back. "A gangster's hideaway. When you promised me a change of scene, Van, you delivered."

"Then you like the room, despite losing your silver dollars?" she asked, smiling.

"I love the room," he answered, "and every last thing in

it." He was looking toward Jill. "Silver dollars are the easiest thing in it to give up."

They all smiled at what Johnny was saying under his words. Van and Nicky beamed, delighted to see their star performer pleased with everything from his accommodations to someone special to share them with.

Johnny grinned, feeling at home with his friends, enjoying these moments of casual socializing that would surely evolve into a profoundly private meeting of hearts and minds when Van and Nicky left.

Jill watched them from her station by the empty game table where five crumpled cards had fallen face up to reveal four of a kind, a Jack of every suit in the deck.

Her hand felt empty where the big circle of a silver dollar had pressed like living fire but moments before. Her heart felt hollower still.

She had to get home. She had to get back to Glory Hole as fast as she could to ask Spuds and Encyclopedia and Wild Blue and Pitchblende and her grandfather about a train robbery—and a man named Jersey Joe Jackson.

♦ Chapter Nine ♦

At the door, the toe of Van's neat pump stubbed a wrinkle in the rug, a white, oblong, envelope-shaped wrinkle.

"What's this?" She bent automatically to retrieve it, but Nicky reached down to restrain her wrist.

"Kid gloves," he advised, half under his breath.

Jill, forgotten at the game table, watched three sets of eyes interweave too-knowing glances. Nicky pulled his silk handkerchief from its purely decorative post at his breast pocket and bent to pinch the missive between its folds before he picked it up.

The trio gathered around the desk while Nicky applied the vintage brass letter opener to cheap, crackling paper.

Van was the first to digest the note's contents. DON'T MISS A SWAN SONG FOR JOHNNY DIAMOND. TOMORROW NIGHT AT THE CRYSTAL CURTAIN. Then—FINAL CURTAINS FOR JOHNNY. A FAN

Van whispered the words as she deciphered the crazy-quilt letters, not linking their meaning into a threatening whole until the signature.

Nicky stormed to the suite's door and jerked it open. "Hey, what you guys been doin' out there, contemplating your navel oranges or what?"

Two shocked Fontana brothers stuttered in their own defense as Nicky waved the letter, still pinioned between the airy folds of his handkerchief.

"Where'd this come from? It wasn't here when Van and I came in."

Giuseppe shrugged while Aldo nibbled his mustache.

"We were here, Nicky," defensive elder brother insisted to angry youngest brother. "Except"—Aldo hit Giuseppe a numbing blow to the bicep—"this goof-off wanted to stroll to the end of the hall to see the Caesars Palace fireworks. We were only gone a minute, maybe—"

"A minute was enough." Nicky's tones dripped contempt. "Some bodyguards. It could have been a, a bom—" Van's warning hand squeezed his forearm. Nicky glanced to Johnny looming over them in the doorway. "It could have been worse," he finished lamely.

"We'll take it to the police first thing in the morning," Van promised Johnny.

"Yeah." Now Nicky oozed confidence. "Not to worry, Johnny boy. I'll, uh, call a Family conference. This is beginning to look like a job for Uncle Mario."

Aldo and Giuseppe hung their dark heads. Aggravating Nicky was one thing. Being judged derelict in duty by Macho Mario Fontana was quite another.

"Don't think anything of it, Johnny." Van used the soothing, unruffled tones of a hotel manager. "You're safe here. It was only a fluke that this . . . this letter slipped through. We'll make sure it doesn't happen again."

Johnny gestured fatalistically at the paper pinched between Nicky's careful fingers. "According to that note, it isn't necessary for it to happen again. Not after tomorrow night."

"Hush." Van leaned up to kiss his cheek. "Nicky will take care of it," she whispered loud enough only for the three of them to hear. "Nicky won't let anything happen to you."

"I guarantee it," Nicky himself promised. "I also guarantee to find some brothers whose brains move a little faster than the average glacier to guard you from now on."

Johnny was shutting the door, nodding wearily, looking

as if believing them were becoming quite a strain.

"Goodnight," Nicky said uneasily while Van, openly distressed, looked on wordlessly and his brothers did their best to swallow their Adam's apples.

The door was almost shut when Johnny heard three firm footsteps. Jill stood beside him, jacket on and fringe swaying, her hat crammed on her head.

"You're not leaving, too?"

"You make it sound like the party's ending." She didn't look up at him, instead focusing leadenly ahead. "Sure, I'm going. I've got to get . . . home."

For the first time in Jill's life, she choked on the word "home." The effort of saying it wrapped the syllable around her tonsils like a sidewinder snake around a desert rat, squeezing all the life out of the word.

Jill had never apologized to anybody for her isolated, off-beat upbringing. Now, a thousand pieces of stolen silver chimed in her brain, changing everything. They even changed how she felt—how she dared to feel—about Johnny.

She stared at him as at a stranger. A vertical furrow plowed between his sandy eyebrows. The amber eyes looked opaque, like yellow fog.

"Jill, please." His hand on her arm restrained her from going. "Tonight, of all nights, I should let you—make you—go. And I . . . Just stay. A while. A little while."

"Johnny, you don't understand!" She tried to pull loose but he wasn't playing Gentleman Johnny now. He didn't let go. The lion's claws had finally come out, and she was caught in them. "It's for your own good that I need to leave now! I've got no right—"

"It's for my own good I need you to stay, Jill!" Emotion poured into Johnny's voice, too much for Jill to ignore, even in her own rush to run and hide fresh wounds.

"Is it . . . those threatening notes, Johnny? I saw you three fussing over that paper."

"My anonymous love letters," Johnny intoned bitterly, as if the words ought to come capitalized, like a title. "It's dangerous selling dreams, Jill. Sometimes people actually buy them. They buy your kind of dream and make it into their kind of nightmare."

"Hey!" He stopped to study her upturned face, abrim with unfocused worry. "That note's nothing," he reassured her. A popular singer had to be as much actor as vocalist. "More of the same old empty sound and fury. Van and Nicky are handling it. It's just that—"

Johnny lifted Jill's hat by the finger dents in the crown. He carefully perched it atop the corset-shaped shade, then gave her a testing look.

The sight of the battered hat atop the racy lampshade made her grin. Johnny smiled back.

"Don't worry about any of that, out there, Jill. It's out there, and we're in here. Don't worry about how the cards fall in casinos across town, or how diplomatic relations are going in Mozambique, or which Fontana brother has the mustache."

He took her hand and led her back across the living room to the bedroom door, where they'd been heading before they were interrupted. "I've made love to you, with you, and I meant it. But tonight's different. Tonight, I need you, Jill, I really do. Don't ask me why. I can't say. But believe me."

She followed him into the bedroom, awestruck, as if invited into the darkest depths of the lion's den.

Cold type in crude patterns zigzagged through the screen

of Johnny's mind. Something dark and shadowy fanned like batwings at his temples. Cold sweat mingled with the afterglow of lovemaking.

Just as Jill, Johnny finally believed something about himself. He'd never been panicked by the anonymous note-sender, not he, Gentleman Johnny Cool. He'd never seen himself as being vulnerable, or the spotlight as anything but a warm, beneficent, money-engendering, ego-salving arena.

Now he saw it could be the death of him, and worse, the death of his newborn love for Jill. Now he had something to save, something to lose. Now, he was scared.

♦ ♦ ♦

"Nicky'll have our scalps! We're not supposed to leave your door for a single second! If he finds only one of us on duty tomorrow morning—" Giuseppe shuddered artistically, even his fine Italian hands trembling slightly.

Johnny filled the doorway with his presence, as he did any stage he stood on.

"It's morning, almost broad daylight. Nobody will bother me. Follow her," he repeated, demand underlining his voice. The ghost of Jill's recently retreating figure still lingered in the hallway. "Try again. Find out where she lives."

"Johnny! She lives in some godforsaken arroyo, in some waterless desert wash. On the dark side of the moon, for all we know! You don't 'find' Jill O'Rourke. She finds you—if she wants to."

"You want to keep me happy? Find her. I need to be able to find her, whether she wants me to or not."

"Nicky will—"

"Forget what Nicky will do, for once! Worry about what

160

I'll do." Johnny's amber-hard eyes softened. "Please, guys. I know what's best for me. I'll make it right with Nicky and your godfather Mario, and the pope if I have to!"

"Okay, okay." Giuseppe was pulling car keys, attached to a somewhat dingy rabbit's foot, from his pocket. "But this is gonna be murder on my suspension system."

"So will I if you don't go," Johnny promised with an incontestable glint in his eye.

Morning painted the desert with a mixed palette of ochers, browns, and muted greens. The sky was a static mirror, reflecting the gently rolling land's hummocks in snowy foothills of cumulus clouds.

Jill stared at the spring, at the still, miraculous surface of fresh water in the middle of an alkaline wasteland. A centuries-old salt cedar tree, massive spreading branches tufted in feathery buff sprays, leaned willowlike over the water.

No mountain lion prowled here today. The only tracks were sneaker treads made by daring weekend tourists who had turned this piece of natural bounty into an impromptu picnic site. Jill bent to pick up a Wonder frankfurter bun package, crushing the wrapper's primary-colored polka dots into her jacket pocket.

She sighed. "Johnny," she whispered, as if to introduce him to this place where he'd never been, to his wild alter ego prowling unseen among the farther rocks. Nothing answered.

She turned and made for the Jeep, parked at a precarious angle on the slope above her. She would have to go back, to her past, to Glory Hole and confront her grandfather. She would have to confront them all and live with the answers.

♦ ♦ ♦

The pint whiskey bottle was brown glass in the way of whiskey bottles immemorial. Its label was half peeled off, and it lurched drunkenly atop the gulch lip, even though it had long since been emptied.

The sun, directly overhead, shone down on everything like an over-achieving spotlight.

Jill held the revolver at arm's length, both hands cupping the butt, her forefinger ready to squeeze the trigger. She sighted down the barrel, a little to the left of target as this gun's quirks required.

Her arms and hands extended level and steady. Her eyes squinted as she held her breath so as not to shake her aim. Still, focusing through tears came hard. She pulled the trigger anyway, slow and certain, ready for the recoil that shuddered up her joint-locked arms.

The whiskey bottle exploded obligingly, spraying shards of what resembled raw topaz over the sand-polished desert floor. Jill moved two steps left and focused on the next whiskey bottle.

"Jilly."

She aimed through the hot veil before her eyes, no worse than the visible sheets of heat boiling off the highway asphalt, and squeezed, squeezed, squeezed the trigger. Glass shattered, the gun's explosion sounding like a jet crashing through the sound barrier. You heard them sometimes, jets from the air base to the north, on the forbidden part of the government firing range they all lived far too close to.

"Jilly!"

She let her straining arms lower the weapon. If she heard anything at all through her waxen earplugs, her grandfather must be shouting.

162

"Jilly, clean that pink guck out of your ears and listen to your grandfather."

Eightball came up beside her. Together they eyed the glass-bestrewn hillside that had served as a firing range since before Jill had come to Glory Hole. Glass shards gleamed like emeralds, diamonds, and topazes in the sunlight.

"You lied to me, Grandfather," Jill said, her voice flat, as she took out one earplug. She had never called him grandfather before. Eightball winced. "You all lied to me."

"We did not. It wasn't so much lying as not tellin' the truth. There's a difference."

"Only in courts of law." Jill lowered the gun on the makeshift shooting table and slammed new bullets into the chamber. "You lied to me about why we were out here, about why I grew up here.

"I thought you all lived way out here because you had to," she went on. "Because the real world wouldn't make any place for you in it. But you lived here because you're just like all those people in Las Vegas you spit at for their flashy ways. You lived here because you were greedy! You're thieves, Grandfather! All of you. Those silver dollars didn't belong to you, not when you stole them off that train in 1943 and not now when you're wasting your lives looking for where they were hidden over forty years ago!"

"Jilly, if you'd jest listen. Encyclopedia told you—"

"Oh, yes." She turned toward him at last, seeing much better because the tears were now streaming down her cheeks. "I know. It's not the money, it's the principle. It's a matter of curiosity. Oh, how could you? To go and steal something and then lose where you hid it? You're not only thieves, and lying thieves, but incompetent thieves!"

"Now, see here, Jilly. We're not liars," he insisted

163

starchily. "When you came roarin' in here at cock's crow this morning with blood in your eye, we all sat right down with you and admitted it all."

She rolled her eyes and shook her head so the tears scattered.

"We told you," he insisted. "The war came up. And Pitchblende got caught, but all he got was a five-year sentence. And Wild Blue was drafted. And Hezekiah moved into Vegas and became a mogul. We could never get to him after that, and he's the one that drove out to Lost Camel Rock and buried the stuff. So naturally we lost track of it. That's why we got a right to find it, to satisfy ourselves. We know it's out there, on the desert. Besides, those silver dollars were loose change back then. They weren't worth more'n five dollars apiece. Now—"

"Now they're worth as much as ten thousand dollars apiece! Can it, Grampa. That's the whole Mojave Desert out there." Jill gestured grandly to the horizon, shimmering mauve in the distance. "Finding those silver dollars is like looking for even odds on the Strip. Hopeless. I don't care if you five over-aged desperadoes sift the sand through the eye of a newt looking for those coins! It's not that, none of that, but the fact that you stole them way back when. It ruins everything. If you're a lie, I'm a lie. And I'll have to lie for you now, but now there's someone I can't lie to, not even by omission."

Her grandfather was silent. Jill rolled the chamber back into place. A stream of spit, brown as a grasshopper's, arched past her cheek to splatter on a flat rock.

"Someone?" Eightball chewed on that with his tobacco. "Some man. That's why you've been coming home so late. Or early, I guess it is."

She was silent.

"That's one of those there 'sins of omission,' too, I reckon," he went on. "You didn't exactly invite us to the weddin'."

"There is no wedding! I never expected a wedding!"

She was tear-blind again and turned to the waiting bottles, shooting true to prove her tears wrong. "People don't do things like that, hardly at all anymore. I'm not a fool. I don't expect things. But I do expect to be able to mean what I say, to be able to hold my head up."

Jill jammed in the earplug, aimed, squeezed, and blew another bottle to smithereens. Her grandfather removed the plug and replaced it with more of his words.

"If he's worth his salt—and these modern fellows that make a girl think weddings are old hat don't strike me as anything to write home about—now, don't glare, Jilly, and mind where you're pointing that pistol! If he's a good man, he won't care what we old fossils did forty years ago."

Jill's mouth was grim. "Probably not. But I do. You can't change that, and I can't change it. Why'd you have to drag me into it, or out to Glory Hole? Why?"

Her grandfather squatted on sand, as he did when he tired of standing. He tired of standing a lot these days.

"I was the last to come out here. It was after your grandmother died. The folks in town, they had some fancy name for you. 'Orphan,' it was. Seems a grandfather isn't worth much when it comes to raising a youngster. Anyway, there was this child protection agency man gonna take you away to some institution, just like that, because it'd be 'better' for you. So you and I came here. That's why we never tried to put you through school or nothing. We figured if they found you, they'd keep you. That's all. We didn't have to hide. Hell, people'd forgot about those old silver dollars by then. It was history. But you were a 'case' on somebody's official books, and you know how those things hang onto you once they get their teeth in you.

"And since we had to be out here anyway, what would it hurt to look for the money? It got to be something under our skin, you know? We didn't need it. Unless to leave a stake to you."

"That's worse, Grampa! Now you're saying that it's because of me that we're all out here, that you're looking for the money. What am I going to do? I have friends at the hotel. I should tell them what I know. And—" She stopped suddenly.

"What's his name?" Eightball asked quietly.

"No!" Jill turned away, her arms wrapped around herself.

"Is it the 'Jack' you were playing with?"

"No!" She paused, then found holding back the truth was as hard as she'd figured it to be. "Kind of. But he really goes by Johnny."

"You got a last name to go with that yet?"

Startled, Jill contracted further into the cold, confused comfort of her own skin. Her head shook violently, until the back of her black hair shimmied like the fringe beneath it while her grandfather watched.

"Looks like this fellow isn't the soul of frankness, either," he noted softly. "We all got secrets, Jilly, and the older we get the deeper they go and the harder it is to let anyone in on them."

Eightball sighed, spat, and sighed again.

"I don't know what to tell you, 'cept we're all sorry as sin that we disappointed you. There's just one thing I know, and I know it to my boot toes. Don't lie about us to that man you love. Lie about us to the law, to the posse, to the hounds of heaven if you can find it in your heart. But don't lie to this Johnny fellow."

She turned, incredulous, to stare into his pale old eyes.

"If I told him, his friends own the hotel, and they'd be obligated to report it. They're already working with the police over something else. If I told him, it'd be out of my hands, and his."

Eightball's final arc of spit startled a whiptail into a mad dash across the shard-splintered land. His face was as wind-carved and sun-ruddy as the rocks in Fire Valley.

"Do what you have to, Jilly," her grandfather said, his tones colder than spring water. "But don't do that. Don't lie to the man."

◆ Chapter Ten ◆

"What about Jill?" Johnny asked.

"Don't worry about it."

"Nicky, that's what you've been saying for the past twelve hours!"

Johnny turned from the dressing-table mirror, where pancake makeup in a shade of bronze-god tan camouflaged a particularly pale face.

People papered the room—the hotel public-relations woman, Nicky, Van, security personnel, and a man and a woman in police beige.

Johnny slammed down the jar of Base No. 3, and they all jumped.

"Dammit, I can't forget about her! She only knows to come to the elevators at one A.M., or to suite seven-thirteen. Now that you've moved me out of there and surrounded me with uniforms and service revolvers, how'll she find me after the show tonight?"

"The boys'll find her," Nicky soothed.

"What if they miss each other? What if Jill goes to seven-thirteen anyway, and the, the killer is waiting there for me? Have you thought of that?"

"No." Nicky's face puckered, then smoothed. "But I'll dig up another brother to babysit that door too. No problem."

"Nicky, there is a problem! And you don't have brothers enough to solve it. Don't you understand? I—" Johnny glanced at the impassive strangers ringing the room, then back at his stage face in the mirror.

He threw down his makeup towel and lowered his voice.

"Nicky, I love her. If you save me from an assassin and something happens to Jill—even if it's just that she can't find me and slips back into that desert of hers where no one can find her—it's not worth it. She needs to know what's going on."

"How can she?" Nicky asked. "She doesn't even know who you really are."

Johnny, trapped by his own charade, dropped his eyes. Giuseppe, dusty and bad-tempered, had returned that afternoon to report he'd "lost" Jill. Maybe Johnny had, too, he thought. Suddenly Van was standing behind him, shielding him from the spectators.

"Johnny, we love Jill too. She's part of the Crystal Phoenix family. But we worry about you. The police think this madman really is going to try to kill you tonight, and the only way to catch him is to let you go on." Her hand reached for Nicky's. "I don't know. It could backfire so easily."

"I'm not afraid," Johnny said. "Not for me. I want this creep off my back for good. Don't you get it? I've got something important to care about now."

"I get it," said Nicky, his licorice-dark eyes sober. "That's why we gotta lay this poison-pen writer to rest. Then you and Jill can have a future to decide about. But for now, everybody's gotta watch you and forget Jill for a while. She'll be okay."

Johnny shook his blond mane. "The show must go on, right?" he asked bitterly. "Why am I so sure that something's going to go wrong?"

◆ ◆ ◆

Jill was desperately seeking Johnny.

It was nine P.M. and the Crystal Phoenix casino was thronged with people, just as it did at midnight. Why, Jill wondered, in an area so familiar she could walk it blindfolded, couldn't she find the one thing she wanted?

She couldn't even spot a Fontana brother, although hotel security staff was frighteningly evident. There were few blatant tip-offs: a cluster of burgundy uniforms near a service exit, and a constant crackle on the house walkie-talkies.

But Jill knew casinos like a worm knows dirt. Something was wrong. Maybe they'd found out about the Glory Hole Gang and the silver dollars, and wanted to nab her.

Damn. Jill punched her hat down over her ears and studied the milling throngs. She wanted only to see Johnny, to tell him the truth, to apologize for being a living lie. To say goodbye.

She caught Solitaire Smith's eye in the low-population baccarat area and paused by the chrome-and-Plexiglas rail.

"You're here early," the taciturn referee commented as he ambled over.

"I'm looking for a man," she said.

"Still?"

"You come up with anybody that fit my description?"

"I might have. But he's not a player."

"Not a player? Well, this guy isn't a poker player, that's for sure. What is he?"

Solitaire's rare smile erupted for a sickle-moon moment. "He's a minstrel."

"Minstrel? You're putting me on, Solitaire! I'm serious!"

"So am I. I'm always serious."

A walkie-talkie buzzed at Jill's back. She froze, then edged away. "I've got to run. See you."

Ducking into a nearby maze of slot machines, Jill hid among the hordes pumping small change into big-buck money-makers, the one-armed bandits that made Las Vegas rich.

The Leopard Lady, wearing a leopard-skin pillbox hat of early Bob Dylan vintage, a pink tiger-pattern dress and zebra-striped high heels, was cramming quarters into a video blackjack slot. Less visible local landmarks, the elderly ladies who whiled away their golden years nursing free drinks and pumping silver into slot machines until their hands grew horny with calluses, added to the night's relentless noise and rhythm.

Jill threaded through the glittering corridors crowded with sweaty palms, coin-filled paper cups, and empty drink glasses. The people seemed incidental to the ambience.

Over the tops of the machine carousels, Jill could spot the billed tips of security caps, cruising like sharks. She darted for the far wall and down a corridor she never took.

Ahead of her wove a fat black form, knee-high to a cowboy boot.

"Midnight Louie! Are you trying to ditch those establishmentarian types too? Or are you just on the way to the kitchens? Where are we, anyway?"

As if in answer, the cat prodded itself into an unheard-of trot. Curious, Jill followed, turning back to see a shadow bulking at the passage mouth behind her.

Someone called out something, maybe to her, maybe to someone else. She didn't wait around to find out. All she knew is that she didn't know how to find Johnny when she needed him.

Louie's tail whisked around a corner Jill's vision hadn't perceived in the dim service corridor. She dashed after it to find herself suddenly in total darkness.

She paused, her heart beating. Then she moved into deeper dark, banging her ankle on an iron rail anchored to the black-painted flooring. She edged farther into an amorphous fog of undifferentiated darkness, aware of vaguely familiar shapes soaring above her—ropes like ship's rigging, and furled sheets of dusky sail.

Louie had lost her, like his opposite number, the White Rabbit that had led Alice down a rabbit hole. Maybe this was a giant mouse hole, Jill speculated, and Louie was after prey.

But as her eyes adjusted, she spotted murky silhouettes at the farthest fringes of the shadowy space. These night people all seemed to be looking ahead, like passengers on a ship approaching land, so Jill edged in that direction.

One final, warily placed step took her to the brink of light, brought her into a halfway world of blending light and dark. The phantom shipboard she explored resolved its shapes into an equipment-crowded backstage area.

Ahead lay the stage itself, a prowlike thrust stage, lit by multicolored baby spotlights and the incandescent glare of one high-watt follow spot.

In the spotlight's circular bore stood a man, and he was singing. Jill stared, trying to integrate the scene into her sense of reality. The words came through before the image, words magnified by the portable microphone in the man's hand, which his moving lips made love to as the words eased out like syrup over Spuds's morning flapjacks.

The man was singing about the hills going green, about being young and alive. He was singing his heart out to someone named Jean, and it was so pretty and passionate, it made Jill's bones want to melt, her eyes want to cry.

She stood frozen while a cobweb of living darkness curled past her booted calves. The cat, she thought dully, the cat had led her here.

Her recent words came back to haunt her. "I'm looking

for a man." Midnight Louie had taken her at her word when no one else had. He'd found her one. He'd found . . . the right man. The one man. The wrong man for her to see standing in the spotlight singing his soul away for—for them.

He had gone silent now, bowing his leonine head to the golden benediction of the spotlight. On tiers around him, they answered him, first with a whisper and rustle, then applause and shouts, escalating to screams. Tokens flashed in the air between him and them—scarves and flowers and shining jewelry and . . . room keys—tribute that came clanking, tumbling, jumbling, clattering to the night-black stage floor that was already alive with gleaming constellations of diamond-shaped glitter.

"Johnny," they called with one voice. *Johnny—Johnny— Johnny.*

Jill saw it all perfectly, even through her tears. She saw her own unsuspected lie mirrored by a different, calculated, bred-in-bone kind of lie.

She had never pretended to aspire to this, to this artificial, fevered mating of light and dark, sound and sight, audience and idol. She'd never dreamed of challenging Them, all those rich and sure and sophisticated ladies. He was theirs, the Performer in the spotlight, so damn desirable to Everybody that any One with a lick of sense would never dare to call him hers.

Jill backed away. Johnny was dissolving in the soft, tear-filled focus of her eyes into an Everyman chained to his center ring, who'd never had a right to weasel his way into her marrow on false pretenses. How? By pretending he was an ordinary person, pretending she could ever be extraordinary to him. Pretending to be free. Pretending to love.

Goodbye, Jill thought, glad now of Glory Hole to run

back to. Turning, she saw the clustered security caps against a far cinder of light. She twisted back to face the stage where, past the still-descending glitter, she spotted one businesslike glint that rang a warning bell in her mind.

Unbelieving, Jill sighted every instinct she owned on the object rising from the audience section directly across from her. It was a gun barrel, a long, lethal gun barrel focusing steady and precise at the heart of the white-hot spotlight on the stage below.

Jill opened her mouth. The crowd filled it with their cries of "Johnny, Johnny" in hundreds of feminine voices. A scenario melded like a lightning-sent jigsaw puzzle in Jill's mind. The guards, Johnny's safety, the way he was kept cooped up . . . Not mob, but still a target.

The back of Jill's left forearm dashed tears from her eyes and knocked the hat with its obscuring brim off the back of her head in one smooth gesture. Her other hand already gripped the revolver butt.

One arm was up, her other hand moving mechanically to meet it so that the gun barrel became a level extension of her eyesight. She aimed the revolver, as lone and undetected as the weapon across from her. Invisible trajectories crossed like long-distance swords.

The house was dark, the distance defeating. People milled around the wielder of the distant weapon, Jill knew— men, women, innocent bystanders all. She could hardly focus past the stubborn residue of tears.

Jill swallowed. The gunman might be police. He might be holding his fire. He might be infinitesimally squeezing the trigger even now.

In the spotlight, a small far figure moved, black on bright white. It moved to the edge of the audience where the gun waited.

Jill couldn't wait. She had to risk it. Her forefinger squeezed the resistant curl of metal beneath it. Slowly—slowly. A whiskey bottle shimmered into her vision, a brown whiskey bottle with a torn label and one death-dealing black circle in the center of it. A tear of sweat sidled down her forehead.

Jill aimed six hairs left of target to compensate for the sight that pulled right and squeezed until it was too late to stop squeezing.

Without ear plugs, her hearing absorbed the full shattering sound of the explosion. In the dark, the barrel spat flame and smoke. Across the way, people stopped screaming "Johnny" and just screamed. Blurring activity swirled where the other gun had been, mimicking fish in a feeding frenzy.

In the spotlight, the black-clothed figure froze.

Behind Jill, the security caps at the door exploded closer.

She turned, holstering the revolver in her shoulder bag, weaving through the lacings of rope into the darkest part of the backstage area. Glory Hole had just claimed a new fugitive.

◆ ◆ ◆

Overhead fluorescents whitewashed the bland walls of the security chief's office.

The room was crowded with people, but only one was sitting. His face was paler than Johnny's stripped of its makeup, and a sweat-slicked dark forelock fell over his sullen forehead.

His hands were cuffed behind him. Beige-uniformed police bracketed him.

"I was just joking," he said for the eighth or ninth time. "It was a publicity stunt!"

Nicky Fontana held a fat two-inch-long shell between his

thumb and forefinger. "Thirty-eights don't kid."

"I never got off a shot. Some sharpshooter shot the piece right out of my hand."

Nicky nodded to the man and woman in beige. "I got to give your department credit for saving my man. You got a lot of nerve to station a sniper in a crowded theater like that."

The detective on the case fidgeted by the door.

"We didn't, Mr. Fontana. We had that place plastered with undercover officers, but they never fired a shot. They didn't, ah, jump in until Frantini here got knocked over by the shot."

"Then who the hell—?" Exasperated, Nicky turned to scan the room.

Security staff, police, and hangers-on shrugged and shook their heads.

By the door, holding it shut with his tall solid frame, Johnny Diamond stared at the man who wanted to kill him.

"Why?" he asked.

Frantini wasn't about to answer, but the cops had already pieced it together.

"This is one of Ugly Al Fresco's boys. From what we figure, Ugly Al's been trying to irritate the Crystal Phoenix out of business since it opened. There have been chronic riflings of the manager's office and open sabotage. We think they hoped to force you to quit, since you're the hotel's most popular draw. You wouldn't scare, so they decided to eliminate you in a spectacular way."

Van von Rhine, standing small and paler than Johnny in a far corner, shuddered. Nicky went to her, curling an arm around her shoulders, and beckoned to Johnny.

"We better wrap this up and get some rest." He paused at the door and looked back at the cops. "Book him!" he barked in farewell, unable to resist the *Hawaii Five-O* finish.

Laughter released everybody's tension and ushered the trio out into a quiet corridor.

"You can sleep in peace now, Johnny," Van said as they ambled wearily toward the hotel lobby. "The detective assured me that Mr. Fresco won't dare try anything more, now that his ace thug's been caught red-handed."

"But who the devil shot the gun out of his hand?" Nicky wondered. "It had to be a police sniper, and they're just going mum because it was a damn risky thing to do. Not that saving you, pal, wasn't worth a few risks." Nicky patted Johnny on the sweatshirted back. "Van's right. Better rest."

Johnny stood in the lobby and watched the couple walk arm-in-arm to the private elevator to the penthouse. Everybody had forgotten Jill, but he hadn't.

He turned slowly to scan the huge area; his above-average height blessed him with a Cinemascopic view of the casino. No clocks decked its walls; the whole idea was to make its patrons forget day, night, rhyme, reason, and time in a gambling nirvana.

Johnny was about to approach a security station to ask the hour when an effacing presence tugged at his awareness. A man in a burgundy-velvet evening jacket stood quietly watching him from a few feet away.

Johnny moved toward him, puzzled. The guy was smiling slightly, as if he recognized him. Johnny didn't know him from Adam, or even Cain and Abel.

"I stopped backstage after all the excitement," the man said, extending the arm from behind his back.

Johnny started, his nerves reading threat in the gesture, but the hand held only a dusty beige Western hat.

"I found this. It didn't look like a prop. And it didn't

look like anything the police would be interested in. I thought you might like a . . . souvenir."

Johnny snatched the hat, his fingers stroking the stiff felt. A dozen possibilities unreeled behind his eyes. The man in front of him seemed to read every one.

"You think—Jill?" Johnny began.

"I don't think anything. I found a hat. I gave it to someone who might take a passing interest in it, besides the police, who might take a more than passing interest in it. End of story."

"Wait!" The stranger was already fading into the crowd. "Why—who are you? What's your name?"

"Smith," he answered laconically, as if not expecting Johnny to believe that. "And I'd say I'm the last thing *you* should worry about . . . Jack."

Johnny paled at the name. "Where is she?" he asked tersely.

The man's dark head shook. "I don't do predictions. Just find hats and put two and two together. Sometimes."

He was gone for good. Johnny stood, turning the hat around and around in his hands as if he expected to find a clue on the band if he kept circling it long enough.

Then the motion paused. Johnny stood even stiller. He slapped the hat down against his leg hard, so hard a faint plume of desert dust coughed into the air. He spun as fast as a big man can and made for the elevators. He still didn't know the time and couldn't spare a moment to ask.

The seventh floor was empty of everything but closed doors. Johnny moved silently down the thick carpeting, afraid he might be wrong and afraid he might be right. Either way, he had something to answer for.

Room seven-thirteen stood with the door slightly ajar. Perhaps it had been left that way when the hotel staff had cleared him out early that morning. Perhaps Frantini had been prowling around here before trying his luck downstairs. Perhaps . . .

♦ ♦ ♦

Johnny entered slowly, softly, reading familiar shapes in the faint light from the hall. He found and flicked on the corset-shaded lamp. He'd never seen it lit. The scarlet lacings burned luridly against the glowing white shade. It would have made him smile, if someone hadn't tried to kill him tonight, and if someone hadn't tried to save him.

The bedroom was even darker. Johnny made for the night stand lamp between the two slick tongues of twin beds, their chartreuse-satin surfaces reflecting ghosts of the living-room light.

He stumbled against something in the darkness between the twin beds and softly cursed it. It softly cursed him back.

"Dammit, you big galoot! Why don't you watch where you're going?"

"Jill." Johnny twisted the light switch beneath his fingers and crouched to inspect what its pool of light revealed. "I was afraid you'd scooted back to that desert of yours, forever this time!"

The lamplight crowned Jill's dark hair with a circlet of rainbow highlights. The top of her head was almost all he could see. She was sitting with her knees drawn up, her arms hugging them.

"I was heading for Glory Hole, all right, and I wasn't coming back. Ever."

"Then why are you here?" he asked.

"Why are you?" she asked back, giving nothing.

"I thought *you* might be here."

"And if I wasn't?"

"I needed to think. It seemed a good place to do it."

"No, it isn't." She paused a moment. "I wanted to come here one last time. But this place is full of ghosts."

"A ghost of you is better than nothing," Johnny said gently.

"My, don't you talk pretty. I didn't mean those kind of ghosts. I meant the real thing. I came here to . . . hide, but then I saw this thin silver thing—against the living room wall. It looked like it was inviting me in, *smiling* at me. It looked like one of the Glory Hole boys, looking all sorrowful, knowing what I have to do." She took a deep shuddering breath. "Or maybe I killed him, the man with the gun, and he's come back to get me already."

"So you're hiding in the dark. From ghosts. Don't you know that's where they get you best?" Johnny's hands shot out to grab her ribs, and she screamed.

He pulled her upright, fighting.

"Let me go, you lying . . . *minstrel!*" It was the first and worst word that came to her tongue, planted there by Solitaire Smith.

"That I am. But I didn't lie. I just didn't tell you exactly what I did."

"That's the same as lying, and if you don't think so, I know five old men a hundred and fifty-six miles north in the desert who've been doing the same slippery thing for twenty-five years, and they know now that sins of omission are as bad as sins of commission, so don't try to sweet-sass me out of it!"

He plunked her down on one satin coverlet and sat on the opposite one. The beds were so close together, or Johnny's legs so long, that their knees touched. He kept hold of her upper arms, as if afraid she'd bolt.

"Jill, listen. The man who tried to shoot me is in police

custody. He's fine, except for a few finger sprains from when you blew the gun out of his hand. You didn't lie. You must be the best thing with a revolver since Annie Oakley. The police don't believe that anyone could have done what you did, so they aren't even looking for you."

Jill settled down a bit. "Got the gun, did I? That's what I was going for. And he *was* trying to kill you?"

"You saved my life, little as you may think of it—or my occupation."

"It's not your occupation! You sing real nice, from what I could hear." Jill scratched her nose in frustration, unaware that Johnny's eyes warmed to the simple gesture.

"I'm glad you're not a music critic," he said.

"It's just that you're a star. People look up to you, kowtow to you, pay to see you, want you without knowing why. I'd never compete in that game. I can't win it, and, I told you, Johnny"—her changeable eyes had gone green-gray with sadness—"I hate to lose. And I'd hate to lose you more than anything. So I'm, I'm giving you up."

"No, you're not, Jill O'Rourke!" he roared, grabbing her shoulders as if to shake her out of her depression. "You don't give up on things, and you don't want to give up on me. Jill, I love you. I'd been a prisoner of this stardom you think owns me until you marched into this suite and my life. I want somebody who doesn't love Johnny Diamond. He's a front man, a bigger-than-life figure on a billboard. And you do love me, whatever that is now and will be. We have no problem."

"Yes, we do."

Her voice was so solemn that Johnny let his hands fall away. Jill straightened and lowered her shoulders.

"It's why I came here tonight. To see Van and Nicky. To tell them that I know who stole the silver dollars. I know where the thieves are. And I came to see you, to apologize for being what I am. I never lied to you, Johnny. I just didn't know. My grandfather and his sidekicks, they stole all that silver back in 1943. And Hezekiah Jackson buried it, only he never told them where, so they've been searching the desert for it ever since. That's it."

"I guess so." Johnny leaned back on his elbows, squinting thoughtfully at Jill. His face looked more leonine than ever at that angle, with the cheekbones wide and his jaw lean and narrow. "That's quite a story."

"It's true! I just found out today."

"It's been a big day," he observed. "Do you have any idea what time it is? They canceled my last show after you nailed the gunman, and I'm out of sync."

Jill's face made like a full moon, growing round with amazement. "I tell you I'm related to a band of wanted desperadoes, and you just want to know what time it is?"

She shot up the sleeve of her buckskin jacket and glared at the watch face on her wrist. "Eleven-thirteen. Why?"

"Seven come eleven," he murmured. "Good. It's the same day. I might as well make the day bigger." Johnny slipped to one knee before her and spread his arms wide.

Jill eyed him askance. He looked like he was about to launch into the standard rendition of "Mammy."

But he didn't. He didn't sing a word. He said them.

"Jill O'Rourke, I know I'm a liar-by-omission, a big galoot who can't parlay four aces into a winning hand, but I can sing on key, and I do love you and want to marry you. What do you say?"

"You're not only crazy, you're nuts! You must be feeling sorry for me again. Well, don't. Me and the boys can survive whatever the government throws at us."

"I don't want to marry 'the boys.' I want to marry you.

And I want to do it for reasons of pure self-interest. Take pity on me, Jill. I'm feeling sorry for me, and I'll go on doing that until you say yes."

"Now you're laughing at me—"

"Jill, I can't win with you. I know it. You got some cards on you?"

Dazed, she slapped a hand to her jacket pocket and found a familiar small oblong. She pulled out a fresh deck.

"We cut the cards. High card loses, and you marry me."

She frowned as she tore the cellophane off. "That's not the way it usually works."

"Cut," he ordered. She paused. "Afraid?"

She laid the cards on her knees and picked up a slim number, flashing the lowest card first at him, then herself.

A ten of hearts.

"Not bad," Johnny conceded. The deck was stacked with more lower cards than face cards. He plucked a slim section off the top, and showed it to her.

Her expression was impassive and remained so.

"What a poker face! Care to tell me?" Johnny asked.

When she didn't speak or move, Johnny slowly turned the card his way. The yellow-haired Jack of diamonds regarded him with the same poker face Jill presented.

Johnny hooted. "I lose! You win! We get married!" A thought occurred as her features remained as wooden as a cigar-store Indian's. "You do honor your bets, Miss O'Rourke?"

Her lips parted slightly. Her eyes blinked and then narrowed calculatingly, growing as icy as when she was unveiling a full house, aces high.

"I suppose . . . if I did marry you, I could afford to buy into the high-stake games. Deal," she agreed pertly. "You've got yourself a playing partner." She extended her hand on the bargain.

It was brushed aside as Johnny leaped forward, knocking Jill back against the pillow. His lips followed where his body had led, pressing hard on hers, then growing soft and tenderly persuasive.

Jill rolled her fingers into the sweatshirt, pulling him closer, wrapping her arms around him, and smiling so much, it was difficult to kiss him back properly. It would all be all-right—everything, she thought. She and Johnny could handle it between them. As long as there was a "them," there wasn't anything they couldn't face, even themselves and their secret, separate loneliness.

Her fist finally hit his shoulder blade until he broke their kiss and she could talk.

"I do like the way you play your cards, Jack, but you have terrible taste in beds! This pillow has got the Rock of Ages buried in its feathers. It's killing me!"

"We'll get rid of it," Johnny promised, pouncing on the pillow and snatching it up. "We'll pulverize the offender!" He loomed over her on his knees, wrenching off the silver satin pillowcase and tearing at the old-fashioned ticking. "Nothing shall harm my bride. Take this! And that!"

Jill giggled helplessly while ticking tore and feathers flew, regaling her like slow, gigantic flakes of snow.

"Ow! That hurt!" Jill pulled the offending flakes off her face. It was a fat, multi-folded piece of stiff paper. Jill lifted one corner. "It's a map. Do you suppose it's *the* map, to the silver?"

"Probably." Johnny plucked it from her hands and set it on the nightstand. "We'll worry about it later. In the meantime—" He shook the empty pillow ticking and goose down wafted over her face.

"I've been involved in something like this before," Johnny mused, watching feathers fly. "But this time I intend to enjoy it."

His lips floated down to pause feather-soft over hers, then he reached out to turn off the light. The darkness that smothered them brought warmth and love and perfect privacy. And no ghosts whatsoever.

♦ Chapter Eleven ♦

"It's always Christmas in Las Vegas," Jill said, leaning out over the Crystal Phoenix rooftop railing. "All that red and green and blue neon twinkling year-round. I don't know how they manage to make it look more Christmas-y for Christmas, but they do."

"Don't fall off," cautioned Darcy, hooking long fingers into the back of Jill's black satin belt.

"I know how to take care of myself," Jill reproached mildly, but she turned her back on the midnight light show along the Strip to study the people still lingering by the penthouse's sliding glass doors.

Darcy rested her long arms on the railing and hunched her lean form down so she spoke near Jill's ear. "Do I smell a smidgeon of that 'Rainforest Civet' perfume on you tonight?"

" 'Jungle Cat,' " Jill corrected. "I put it on with a ladle. Do you think it's too much?" She sniffed worriedly at her bare wrists while Darcy shook her head tolerantly.

"How are things going at the new house?" Darcy asked next.

"Terrific! I tell you, between following construction on that and running out to Glory Hole to see how Grampa and the boys are doing with their 'Ghost Town, Landmark Mine and Treasure Tour' set-up keeps me too busy to sit up nights and play poker."

"Living in a house is nice." Darcy turned back to the lights. "I love Steven's little place in the desert." During a pause, Darcy glanced sideways at Jill. "When are you going to tell him?"

"Tell who? What?" Jill blustered.

Darcy shrugged. "I've always wanted to be a godmother."

Jill's fist chucked her shoulder. "Darcy McGill Austen, you breathe one syllable of what you're thinking to Johnny and I'll . . . do something drastic."

Darcy just shrugged. After a silent minute, Jill turned to view the glittering nightscape again.

"He'd . . . get all funny and old-fashioned and stuff. You find out these things awful soon nowadays. I liked the old days when a lady could just wear her aprons high, get on about her business, and let her knitting habits tell the tale."

"Jill, you don't wear aprons and you don't knit. You do get on about your business, but this is Johnny's business, too. After all, you've been married six months now."

"Hush, Darcy. It's Grampa and the boys. Johnny'd never let me ramrod out to Glory Hole by myself in the Jeep if he knew. He'd hog-tie me to some doctor's waiting room the whole time. And Eightball and the boys need me, maybe more'n Johnny does right now. They're building a whole new life for themselves out there."

"At least the Spectre Mountain Gang has found something else to do," Darcy mused, "even if it's the last thing Las Vegas needs, another tourist attraction."

"This is going to be different, Eightball says, an authentic tourist attraction. I guess it was all that publicity about them and Glory Hole that gave them the idea. What a bunch of hams! But it's not easy for them to deal with the real world by their lonesomes. I've got to act as translator, you know?"

"You always did take care of them; they're lucky."

"They're lucky they didn't go to jail," Jill added grimly. "It took Nicky, Van, Johnny, *and* Uncle Mario to engineer that one. And I'm going to see that they keep on behaving like model, money-earning citizens so nothing comes back to haunt them."

"You mean like the phantom of the Ghost Suite?"

"Pshaw, Darcy, you don't want to kid about a thing like that."

"Oh, that's Van's crazy superstition, Jill, and now you're half believing it."

"I saw something in that room that last night, honest, I did. I'm glad Van's closed it again permanently. Jersey Joe Jackson and his room don't belong to us, our time. Never did."

"Maybe I'll use it for a story," Darcy mused. "Or give the idea to Steven. Now that he's on number thirteen of the Nightcrawler series, he could use some fresh backgrounds."

"Honestly, I'm surrounded by famous writers and singers and hotel owners. I wish I did something special."

"Don't say that to Johnny; he'd tell you that making the final round in the World Series of Poker is pretty special."

"Only winning counts," Jill said flatly.

Darcy turned back to face the rooftop. "Only living and loving counts," she said. "On that score, I'd say you and I've done pretty well for ourselves."

Against the patio doors, back-lit by a warm glow of interior lights, silhouettes instantly identifiable to the two women moved slightly.

There was Van von Rhine's tiny, feminine form, and Nicky Fontana's flailing figure as his hands kept eager pace with his words.

A pipe protruded from one tallish male silhouette's profile; Darcy's eyes grew becomingly soft as they dwelled on it.

Jill's eyes ignored the rest, skillfully cutting her favorite from the herd: the tallest figure, a massive yet lithe man even now tipping New Year's champagne into almost-empty glasses.

Jill ran her hands over her long, tartan plaid taffeta skirt. "I'm not used to this holiday rig, especially when it runs all the way to the floor."

"Your dress is lovely; Johnny must like to see you in something other than jeans now and again."

"Yeah . . . but then it's usually nothing. You're right; I will have to tell him soon." Jill grinned and drained her champagne glass of ginger ale in one, endless, Eightball-approved swallow. "Waiter!" she called, raising her empty glass.

"Girl talk done?"

Johnny ambled over to fill their empty glasses, but only Darcy accepted the champagne.

"What were you two plotting?" he asked.

"Steven's next book," Jill answered promptly.

Darcy squeezed her arm and pulled away from the railing. "Speaking of which, I'd better fill him in on what we've got planned for him." In seconds she became another vague yet warmly familiar silhouette against the inside lights.

Johnny tucked himself around Jill, his arms wrapping her in at the railing. "It's kind of cold way out here, half-pint," he noted, running warm hands up her bare forearms. "Almost January."

"Not until tomorrow," Jill said. "What time is it?"

"Almost midnight. Almost next year."

She put down the empty champagne glass while Johnny watched her, aware that she had become a source of as-yet-unshaped curiosity for him. Unshaped was right, she thought, seeing the New Year advancing on her in a plump, diapered form.

"It should be an interesting year," Johnny was saying. "I'll be living in a real house for the first time in twelve years. It's too bad the boys insisted on staying out in the desert instead of coming into town to celebrate. I kind of miss the old buzzards now and again. Marrying you is like acquiring five Dutch uncles too."

"They're happier out there," Jill said. "Johnny."

"Yes, sweet? What's worrying you?"

She impatiently tugged on his sleeve. "What time is it? I don't want to miss the New Year."

"Not yet. I'll let you know. What is so important about this New Year anyway?"

"It's . . . our first. And I don't trust that six-grand Rolex of yours to keep time."

"You mean that six-grand Rolex of Aldo's," Johnny chuckled. "It's a pity I gave up poker."

"No, it isn't. It's a mercy."

"I could still beat you at a good game of strip poker any day."

"Only if I wanted you to, darling."

"Did you, that first game?"

"Maybe. Maybe not. That's for me to know. . . ."

"I know the rest." He turned her from the railing to face him.

Behind them, Nicky sang out, "Okay, folks—it's coming! Nineteen eighty-seven. Bottoms up and lips puckered!"

Fireworks sparkled against the star-spangled sky. Distant revelers blew paper horns. Far away, church bells rang out their solemn celebration.

On the rooftop of the Crystal Phoenix, six people cheered and hugged each other.

"Look at them," Van said, suddenly sober. Darcy and Steven and she and Nicky paused in their respective marital embraces. "Newlyweds," Van diagnosed fondly.

"Hey, we're not exactly oldlyweds," Nicky objected.

But Johnny and Jill stood alone with each other, limned by the soft rooftop illumination against the limitless velvet night. There was good long distance between her upturned profile and his downturned one, but their rapt expressions seemed to bridge it.

Johnny bent and Jill stretched until their lips met, merging silhouettes. They broke apart gently, then Jill pulled Johnny farther down still, until her lips reached his ear, where they remained a minute or more.

His head jerked up. They were both on their natural, widely differing levels again, motionlessly regarding one another. Then Johnny yelped a mixture of surprise and joy and lifted Jill high in his arms, up over his head, whirling her around.

"I remember when you used to do that," Van mused to Nicky.

"You were smaller then," he answered defensively. "Besides, I'm a major Vegas hotelier now. I got to maintain my dignity."

"Newlyweds," Darcy explained again. She linked her arm through her husband's. "Isn't that right? I bet he even recites poetry to her."

"I doubt it," Steven answered in his calm professorial baritone. "He sings his poetry. And I bet he doesn't know the Cavaliers from Rod McKuen."

"Hey!" Nicky was intrigued. "The Cavaliers! Didn't they split off from that funky New Wave rock group, Surface Tension?"

"Not in this century," Darcy said. "Oh, those two are so romantic. . . ."

"They'll get over it," Nicky promised.

"Hey!" He whistled shrilly. "Romeo and Jilliet! Come on in. It's getting cold out here and the New Year's officially in. We better find something respectable to do indoors."

Hand in hand, Jill and Johnny broke away from the darkness and moved into the light beside their friends.

"What do you have in mind?" Johnny asked.

They all looked at Van, who played the hostess to perfection.

"I don't know . . . how about bridge?" she proposed playfully.

"What's bridge?" Jill asked.

A sudden, pregnant silence fell over the group.

"Do you mean," Nicky asked, "that you don't know how to play bridge?"

"Oh, is it a card game, then? No, Eightball never taught me . . . bridge. How does it go?"

Nicky swept an avuncular, larcenous arm around Jill's waist and started ushering her through the open sliding glass doors.

"So you don't know how to play bridge . . . Come right along. Better not miss this, Johnny. My friends and I are going to take your little card-shark bride to the cleaners."

Johnny, the last in, turned back to the night to draw the sliding door shut. He smiled to himself before joining them. "Wanna bet?"

♦ Midnight Louie Has a Close Encounter ♦

At least I am left to myself after all the excitement and am allowed to resume my afternoon snoozes in my favorite suite, seven-thirteen.

I slip into the Crystal Curtain every now and again to catch my favorite crooner, Gentleman Johnny Diamond, in his revamped act, which features an enlarged repertoire and various innovations, all going to show you can teach an old dog new tricks if you give him the proper incentive. And Miss Jill O'Rourke is the proper incentive—in spades— for Gentleman Johnny Diamond.

I am somewhat miffed that no one invites me to visit the famed vicinity of Glory Hole, now that the newspapers are full of the ghost town's name again. It is quite the seven-day wonder. The Glory Hole Gang get all their aging mugs in the local rag, and there is much talk of prosecution and finding lost treasure.

But it turns out that the old map Miss Jill O'Rourke places her pretty ear upon so rudely in suite seven-thirteen is for the most part indecipherable, being full of obscure notations that mean nothing to anybody, least of all the gentle old coots from Glory Hole.

(Not that I wish to hold age against anybody. I myself am more than somewhat past my prime, but my senses are in first-class condition despite it, due to a diet heavy in lean piscine products. I am not so debauched as to engage in jogging, as do other physical fitness buffs of my generation, but I am known to break into a gentle trot now and again to evade an overzealous acquaintance,

193

particularly Chef Sing Song when he is in the mood for avenging missing carp.)

Of course, it turns out that the old fellows are not liable to wither in stir, as something the legal eagles call a "statue of limitations" is expired. (I am all for artwork if it is useful in the administration of justice, and I see no sense in punishing these long-in-the-fang gentlemen for a misdoing perpetrated so long ago, particularly in which they have no gain.) In all the hullabaloo over the so-called Silver Hoard and the Glory-Hole-Gang and the Hotel-Singer-Shot-At headlines, once again it is overlooked that Midnight Louie has his fine feline paw in the happy outcome.

I ask you, am I not alert? Do I not lead Miss Jill O'Rourke and her primed forty-five to the backstage area?

Does anyone doubt that, save for me, Gentleman Johnny would not be singing anywhere today, except in a celestial chorus?

This may be a noble end, and I'm sure the heavenly trillers could use a good baritone, most of whom usually end up doing a hot riff in the other place, if you know what I mean, but this is a stiff, pardon the expression, price to pay for the bad taste of allowing events to take their preordained course without a bit of delicate intervention on my part. After all, what do they pay me for, except to point my erring friends in the right direction?

And I do not put much credence in the notion of heavenly intervention—i.e., the phantom of long-planted Jersey Joe Jackson taking a benign interest in the romance burgeoning by the light of his corset-shaded lamp or supposedly revealing the partial hoard of silver dollars and a useless map via the suite bed linens.

It strikes me that genuine spirits have better things to do than to air dirty laundry in public—their own or anyone else's. Also, I do not subscribe to ghosts. It is not that I have not seen many things of an outre nature in Las Vegas, the least of which is watching Hester Polyester on a roll at the craps table, but I find attributing the outcome of purely human events to the intervention of non-human agencies a highly suspicious tendency and plain wishful thinking.

But then I am an old Las Vegas hand and know how things go down in this town. At this time I am fairly satisfied that I have the Crystal Phoenix ship-shape and smooth-running, with no likelihood of any more untoward events of an adventuresome or even a vaguely romantic nature.

After all, I have been instrumental in three weddings in less than two years and am ready to rest upon my laurels. It is precisely this I am doing in suite seven-thirteen, which Miss Van von Rhine is kind enough to declare off-limits to hotel guests and personnel. Me, she does not mention, but I like a low profile.

In fact, I am curled up on a chartreuse satin pillow. My, er, fingers, so to speak, making neat puncture marks all over the satin in rhythmic motions. I am humming to myself—I have a deep, thrilling baritone myself, to hear certain of my many ladyfriends both human and feline tell it— when my eyes slip semi-shut.

I am a past master of the semi-shut look-see, and many a wrongdoer is caught out because he takes me for a statue (not of the limitations variety). So when this slim silver dude—and I mean silver from his slicked-back hair to his two-tone 1943 wingtips; I am talking Tin Woodsman here—sort of slides out of the long silver-satin drapes against the wall and into the corner of my eye, naturally I am skeptical.

Apparently this specter does not see so good, as it walks right through the sofa on my left and goes to the bedroom. By surreptitiously keeping my eyes peeled to the side—a talent useful for snagging small snacks of the rodent family—I can see this swamp-gas dude is smiling, right through the back of his head!

Then he turns as if to say goodbye (I am imaginative from the time I was a wee nipper) and winks at me!

I tell you, I am an unshakeable dude by nature, but it is enough to make the hairs stand up on the back of my neck—and tail. It is a good thing I am not the superstitious sort, or I would avoid myself like the plague. Of course, I know I am dreaming and luckily am awake enough to realize that fact.

But I swear off Scotch in my milk from that moment on.

♦ Tailpiece ♦

The Plot Thickens,

But Louie Still Gets Slim Regard

Once again I have been confined to little more than a cameo role. However, I am happy to see the Treasure of the Spectre Mountains taking a bigger role in the action.

A lot of the Glory Hole Gang material was cut in this book's first incarnation, along with Chef Song and the Fontana brothers. The New Year's Eve scene that reprises the couples from the earlier two novels was also chopped. Since one of my major aims in the Quartet was creating colorful continuing characters, it's no surprise that I continued some of them right into your current mystery series, Louie.

I am all for the Revenge of the Cut Characters, since I have been one of them myself. I understand that some readers are particularly partial to Fontana Inc. Besides being mad about myself, of course.

Yes, they are, and it's not easy to write a Gang of Nine. In your latest Midnight Louie mystery, *Cat in a Jeweled Jumpsuit*, which involves Elvis and Elvis impersonator acts, the Fontana brothers play Full Spectrum Elvis: all the facets of the King at various stages in his career.

I also notice that although the Quartet is supposedly a romance series, I have been given no leading lady here, though I do have my paws full of feline femininity in the mystery series. What gives? Where are the delicious dames and treacherous tootsies of the feline persuasion?

197

You were supposed to keep a low-profile here. And, quite frankly, I hadn't thought about your social life yet.

Did you miss a sure bet for steamy scenes! Of course I was not, ah, reproductively adjusted yet, so I suppose it would have been irresponsible to show the long-nailed, long-haired ladies fawning all over me.

Speaking of sexual responsibility, I was "daring" for the times in these books. The stringent romance-novel formula then required consummation slightly before the happy ending and resulting marriage, so I made sure to mention that the happy couples used contraceptives. That just didn't work out for Couple Number Three, which is why baby makes three at the end of this book. Although romances are in some respects fairy tales that glide over reality now and then, I felt strongly that this was one area where a little reality was needed. I was just finishing the series as the existence of AIDS became general knowledge. Although suspension of disbelief is necessary to romance and fantasy writing, I'd have been uneasy about writing these books after AIDS became a fact of life. You will notice that sexual responsibility is a theme in your current mystery series. I don't see why crime fiction, with all its gory details about death and autopsies, primly avoids reference to protection from unwanted consequences when characters have intimate relationships.

Do I know about your penchant for sexual responsibility! It nearly cost me my . . . well, I'd rather not go into the gory personal details, being a noir kind of guy who likes to have his fun without much thinking about the consequences. Would Sam Spade? At least you were able to devise a dignified way of pushing me into the Age of Anxiety. So what's up next, pussycat?

A final Crystal Phoenix romance, of course, and the unraveling of exactly what the criminal elements have been pursuing throughout the Quartet. You'll notice that your current series also includes background mysteries and murders.

Goodie. I love to see criminal elements unraveled. Especially by my retractable shivs. Any hints as to the lucky couple up next?

Well, you've met half the equation already.

Hmmm. I just hope I have a bigger role in the penultimate volume.

"Penultimate volume." That's a pretty big mouthful, Louie, but you were never one to think small. The fact is, yours is a never-ending story. Although the Quartet "ended," you went on. I really don't foresee any penultimate volume for you.

That is a relief.

8/00